Who wouldn't recognize his unforgettable eyes?

Lola could just imagine the expressions on the well-bred faces around her were she to denounce their host as a thief.

"Miss Golightly and I," Cesar informed his guests, "have met before—in a previous incarnation. She was Cleopatra, and I was a humble Egyptian slave."

"I hope I had you beheaded," Lola retorted dryly.

"You did." His golden eyes mocked her. "But I got my revenge several centuries later, when you were Marie Antoinette."

"Perhaps I'll turn Portia in this life," Lola threatened tartly, "and have you imprisoned. Burglary, perhaps."

"The only things Cesar steals are women's hearts," an onlooker observed gaily. "But I didn't know you could be jailed for that."

Cesar's eyes were holding Lola's, his gaze startlingly direct....

WELCOME
TO THE WONDERFUL WORLD
OF *Harlequin Romances*

Interesting, informative and entertaining,
each Harlequin Romance portrays an appealing
and original love story. With a varied array
of settings, we may lure you on an African safari,
to a quaint Welsh village, or an exotic Riviera
location—anywhere and everywhere that adventurous
men and women fall in love.

As publishers of Harlequin Romances, we're
extremely proud of our books. Since 1949,
Harlequin Enterprises has built its publishing
reputation on the solid base of quality and
originality. Our stories are the most popular
paperback romances sold in North America; every
month, six new titles are released and sold at
nearly every book-selling store in Canada and the
United States.

For a list of all titles currently available,
send your name and address to:

HARLEQUIN READER SERVICE,
(In the U.S.) P.O. Box 52040, Phoenix, AZ 85072-2040
(In Canada) P.O. Box 2800, Postal Station A
5170 Yonge Street, Willowdale, Ont.   M2N 6J3

We sincerely hope you enjoy reading
this Harlequin Romance.

Yours truly,

THE PUBLISHERS
Harlequin Romances

Never Kiss a Stranger

Mary Gabriel

Harlequin Books

TORONTO • NEW YORK • LONDON
AMSTERDAM • PARIS • SYDNEY • HAMBURG
STOCKHOLM • ATHENS • TOKYO • MILAN

Original hardcover edition published in 1985
by Mills & Boon Limited

ISBN 0-373-02703-6

Harlequin Romance first edition July 1985

CHAPTER ONE

'I NEVER kiss strangers,' Mrs Prenderghast confided icily to Lola. 'One can't tell what one might catch.'

Lola was well-used to such pronouncements from her employer.

'She *is* your publisher,' she replied, watching Madame Roche waddle briskly to her car. The dumpy little woman had been waiting at Nice airport to greet Mrs Prenderghast with a Gallic triple kiss, but Mrs Prenderghast had frigidly declined the salutation—which, Lola had noticed with amusement, owing to Mrs Prenderghast's bulk and Madame Roche's dumpiness, had been offered on tip-toe. Madame Roche had gabbled non-stop all the way from the airport to the imposing front of the hotel, where she had just dropped them off.

'Publisher or not,' Mrs Prenderghast sniffed, 'the woman is *French*.' She made the word sound like some unmentionable condition. Lola smiled. Over the past six weeks, she had had to familiarise herself with Mrs Prenderghast's extensive business connections. Madame Roche, who was waving gaily as she drove away, was the head of a Marseilles-based publishing company which had recently begun publishing Mrs Prenderghast's books in French. The sales, Lola understood, had been very brisk indeed, which accounted for Mme Roche's enthusiasm. But Mrs Prenderghast, as Lola had had ample time to discover in those same six weeks, was a woman of strong views.

'Never kiss a stranger, Lola,' she said firmly.

Some chance of that, Lola thought ruefully, shepherding her employer into the magnificent foyer of the Hotel Grande. She wasn't likely to kiss anybody on this working holiday, let alone some mysterious stranger. The buttoned porter staggered in after them, burdened with hand-stitched pigskin suitcases. Lola was carrying her own bag, which had somehow been ignored in the confusion, and trying to keep an eye on her erratic employer at the same time.

But it didn't take long for trouble to brew at the gleaming ebony reception desk. *That* was predictable.

'But I *always* have Suite 223,' Mrs Prenderghast told the miserable-looking manager in a chilly voice. 'My secretary booked the suite three months ago!'

'An unforgivable mistake, Madame,' the manager said dismally, and pointed to an even less happy-looking clerk. 'This imbecile confused 223 with 225, the one next door, and I regret to tell you that 223 is already occupied by a Bulgarian gentleman. The room was issued only yesterday. Unforgivable, I repeat——' He was a small, balding man. Rubbing his hands unctuously in front of Mrs Prenderghast, who was wearing even heavier and more old-fashioned make-up than usual, and sporting garish corals and pinks, he reminded Lola rather of a minnow confronting the poisonous bulk of a Portuguese man-o'-war.

'Typical,' Mrs Prenderghast snapped to Lola. 'These people can't even carry out the simplest instruction. The country's gone *completely* to the dogs since de Gaulle died.'

'I'm sure it's not as bad as all that,' Lola said

mildly, hoping Mrs Prenderghast wasn't going to start the Napoleonic Wars all over again. 'Can't we have the suite next door?'

'Of course, Mademoiselle,' the manager said, relieved to have someone on his side. 'As soon as we discovered the error, we transferred your booking to Suite 225. It has been made all ready.' He rubbed his hands in Mrs Prenderghast's direction. 'It is, after all, just next door to your usual suite. If you would just condescend——'

'Does it command the same view of the sea?' Mrs Prenderghast asked icily.

'Exactly the same view, Madame——'

'And is it as big?'

'Even bigger,' the manager assured her, hope starting to dawn in his spaniel eyes. 'And, if I may be permitted to say so, even more luxurious and to Madame's exacting taste. I assure you, the Bulgarian gentleman, and not your esteemed selves, is suffering by the exchange of suites.' A nice touch, Lola thought. Mamie Prenderghast was never one to turn down a good bargain.

'I'm not paying a penny extra, mind,' Mrs Prenderghast said sharply. 'You made the mistake, not me.'

'Of course, of course,' the manager beamed, obviously delighted not to have lost so valued—if troublesome—a client as Mrs Prenderghast. As well he might be. Ten days in one of the Grande's best suites was going to cost just under three thousand pounds. Tax-deductible pounds, of course.

'That seems very fair,' Lola hinted. She was dying for a wash. 'Shall we go up?'

'We might as well,' Mrs Prenderghast decided, with the air of a mediaeval monarch conferring life on the wretched manager. 'It's *very* tiresome, but we shall have to put up with it.'

Lola handed over their passports and followed in her employer's wake. One porter was scuttling into the service lift with the pigskin valises (somehow Lola's own bag had been forgotten again) while another accompanied them into the guest lift with the keys.

'Incompetent fools,' Mrs Prenderghast said crushingly as the lift doors closed behind them. The porter, a timid-looking man on the same scale as the luckless manager, flinched under the combined blast of the retort and Mrs Prenderghast's perfume. 'How could they *possibly* give my suite to someone else?'

'It was very careless,' Lola agreed diplomatically. She was just glad to be off the road at last. She smiled soothingly at the porter as the lift whooshed them up to the twenty-second floor. The entire staff of the Grande was probably mobilised to action stations before each yearly Prenderghast arrival.

As the porter ushered them down the corridor to the vast portals of 225, a big man in a dark suit was just opening the door of 223. Lola's heart sank. It was utterly predictable that Mrs Prenderghast should stop dead in her Bruno Magli shoes, and tap the stranger's shoulder with a scarlet-painted claw.

'Excuse me,' she said in a grim contralto. 'You are occupying the suite that should rightfully be mine.'

The stranger turned with lowered brows. He was in his early forties, Lola guessed, and he had a hard face with a massive, rocky nose to go with his hard and massive-looking shoulders. Eyes as cold as wet black pebbles fixed Mrs Prenderghast suspiciously.

'*Pardon?*'

'I want you to know,' Mrs Prenderghast repeated, her voice climbing to its most devasting heights of class-superiority, 'that the suite you are occupying should rightfully be *mine*. Stop *pushing*, Lola,' she commanded as Lola tried anxiously to encourage her past the grim-looking man. 'I have occupied that suite every year for the past twelve years, my man, and this is the first occasion——'

'You are wasting my time,' the rocky man shrugged. He turned to the oak door, and rapped on the number-plate with knuckles like large pebbles. 'This room is mine.' His accent was heavy East-European. And closing his mouth to a lipless line, pushed past Mrs Prenderghast. The width of his shoulders gave him an oddly rolling, sailor-like gait.

He slammed the door indifferently in their faces.

'Well, of all the nerve——' Mrs Prenderghast began, staring at the door with bulging blue eyes, but Lola urged her employer hastily towards the open doorway of 225. The sooner she got Mrs Prenderghast and a daiquiri together, the easier life was going to be all round.

'Let me run you a nice cool bath,' she suggested sweetly. 'You've had such a trying day.' To her relief, Mrs Prenderghast allowed herself to be piloted into her suite. The Bulgarian gentleman had looked a tough customer, even for Mrs Prenderghast to handle.

And the suite, as the manager had promised, was magnificent. Lola stared around in awe; even on the sumptuous scale which Mrs Prenderghast demanded, this was something special. The vast windows in the drawing-room, framed by heavy yellow silk drapes, looked out over a towering view of the beach front and the Mediterranean which stretched out beyond. The furnishings harmonised in a show of rococo magnificence that was, she judged, at least partly genuine.

The carpet was deliciously soft underfoot. The exquisite furniture was all rosewood and bronze gilt. Lola sighed, thinking of the featureless modernity of their Milan hotel. 'This is a beautiful suite, Mrs Prenderghast.'

'If it isn't *exactly* the same as 223,' Mrs Prenderghast said ominously, shooing the porter out, 'I'll skin that manager alive.

'Honestly,' Lola said with a touch of acid, tying back her long, thick blonde hair, which was beginning to be uncomfortably hot on this sultry afternoon, 'I've never known *anyone* make such a fuss about things as you.'

'It's the only way to get things done, dear,' Mrs Prenderghast said serenely, looking around. 'Colour television, cocktail cabinet . . . what the devil's this?'

'A video recorder,' Lola decided.

'Newfangled rubbish. And this?'

Lola studied the space-age object with clear grey-green eyes. Her brother, who loved all things electronic, possessed one. 'I think that's an ionizer. They're supposed to make people feel more alert.'

'I'll have it sent down to the manager, then,' Mrs Prenderghast said drily.

Lola couldn't help smiling as she went to run the bath. There were two bedrooms, one immense, the other merely huge; both had attached dressing-rooms, and both shared the marble-floored bathroom suite.

Mrs Prenderghast pulled off the jacket of her coral suit, revealing a pink silk-clad bust that vied with the rococo ornamentation in the sheer mass of its curve. Mrs Prenderghast, at sixty-six, was a woman of monumental proportions. 'The rainbow galleon,' some unkind newspaper critic had dubbed her on the publication of her twelfth book.

She sailed over to the window, and gazed down at the tiny cars and ant-like people far below. 'I like heights,' she said firmly. 'Prenderghast had no stomach for heights at all. He was in many ways a very weak man.'

'Really?' Not for the first time, Lola felt a pang of pity for the departed Prenderghast. He had borne all the trials of marriage to his wife, so to speak, with none of the compensations. It had been only after his death, some fifteen years before, that Mrs Prenderghast had written the first of the romantic novels which had by now made her one of the richer authors in the publishing world.

'Where shall I put the typewriter?' Lola asked.

'On the table next to the window, sweetie.' Lola heard muscles creak in her shoulders as she hauled the electronic typewriter out of its case, and staggered across the room with it. This job was definitely not in her line. It wasn't the first time she'd thought *that*, either. She'd wanted a pleasant summer job to tide her over the first three months after leaving university, and she'd been delighted when the post of holiday companion to Mamie Prenderghast had come her way. Except that Mrs Prenderghast's 'holiday companions' (and Lola knew now that there had been half-a-dozen before her) had to be a cross between shepherdesses and removal men. A dash of masochism helped.

She'd had to bite back her pride quite savagely at first. Those first few days in Italy, after they'd left London, had been ones of seething anger; Lola Golightly was a spirited young woman, and she'd been seriously irritated by Mrs Prenderghast's casually dictatorial attitude to the world. Lola had had to remind herself more than once that pride was an expensive commodity, and one she was in no position to afford at this stage of her life. She'd needed a job in a hurry, hadn't she? Still, if she'd known what was in store for her on this trip, she'd never have bothered to answer the advertisement in *The Times* three months earlier, asking for a 'presentable young person to accompany mature lady on European tour, adequate remuneration, full travelling exp and board incl.'

In her innocence, she'd imagined some sweet and slightly melancholy old thing having a summer fling in the autumn of her life.

'Not there, Lola,' Mrs Prenderghast commanded, 'I've changed my mind. Put it out on the balcony, where I can see the Mediterranean.'

Lola bit back her retort. It was much too late for regrets now. She staggered out on to the expansive balcony. Anyway, there were only a few more weeks of this royal tour left. And she'd saved up just about every penny of the rather meagre 'remuneration' that Mrs Prenderghast paid her, which was going to be useful when she got back to England, and starting looking for a *real* job.

Besides which, she *was* on the Côte d'Azur. She hefted the machine on to the balcony table, and peered down at the sea, gilded with late afternoon sunlight. Selfish old Tartar that she was, Mrs Prenderghast—known to her many millions of readers as Viola May Banksteads—had excellent taste when it came to hotels and holidays. And she wasn't quite as awful as Lola had at first supposed. Nearly, but not quite. There were flashes of generosity in that vast, colourful bulk.

On the other hand, she could be, on her worst days, a petulant, nagging, hypochondriac monster. Lola had another twinge of pity for the deceased Mr P., and set about unpacking her employer's brightly hued clothing while the lady novelist herself made and sipped a daiquiri on the balcony in anticipation of her bath.

Lola was tall for a woman, almost five-ten, and she carried her height with a taut, slender grace. Well over half of it, her brother Tom had once estimated, was made up of long and beautiful legs. Her eyes were a deliciously rainy grey-green, like her mother's, and her hair was an unusually dark, tawny gold. The honey-brown tan which reflected her mother's Italian origins didn't prevent an untidy sprinkling of freckles across her short, neat nose. There were even two or three on the bruised-satin pink of her lips.

'You know, Lola,' Mrs Prenderghast said, coming back inside, and unfastening the chunky diamond earrings which sparkled so brightly against her vivid red rinse, 'I think I'm going to have to kill Armand.'

'That would be a pity,' Lola smiled.

'No, he's getting in the way, and I'm rather sick of his sinister good looks. Besides, it has to come sometime, to make way for Terry. The only question is how. What would you recommend? A fall off a cliff?'

'A gruesome accident at a level-crossing,' Lola said firmly. 'The car crushed almost beyond recognition.'

'Excellent idea. Blood everywhere. That'll serve the blighter right.' Mrs Prenderghast scribbled a note in her crocodile-skin note book. Her latest novel, *Unquenchable Flame of the Heart*, was nearing completion. Lola's private opinion had always been that Viola May Banksteads' books were unreadable rubbish, but *Unquenchable Flame* was going to sell an easy three million; it dripped with what Mrs Prenderghast (and her predominantly teenage readers) obviously thought was torrid sex. The doomed Armand, for example, had muscularly raped the virginal heroine no less than five times by the end of Chapter Three. It was part of the Banksteads formula, though, that the muscular lover should come to a grisly end in Chapter Twelve, so that the heroine could reconcile herself to marrying the honourable but un-sexy hero in Chapter Fourteen.

'You shouldn't leave your diamonds lying around like that,' Lola warned, her frugal instincts jangled as she watched her employer casually pile bracelet, brooch and earrings into a glittering heap worth about ten thousand pounds on the coffee-table.

'All insured,' Mrs Prenderghast said airily. 'Besides, there's only you to steal them, sweetie. And they'd catch you in no time. Unfasten me.'

Five minutes later, her coppery coiffure restrained by a lilac bath-cap, Mrs Prenderghast sank her pink bulk into a frothy, cool bath.

And Lola relaxed for the first time since leaving Milan.

She unpeeled the plain khaki dress which had been sticking to her back all day, despite the lightness of the material, and clad only in panties and bra, lifted her arms luxuriously to the cool breeze from the balcony. They hadn't had too much sun on the holiday so far; she was going to have to beware of the seventy-four freckles (as a girl she'd once unhappily counted them all) waiting to appear on her fine skin.

Those freckles, together with unfashionably full breasts and a total lack of vanity, had persuaded Lola to go to university, rather than take her beautiful body to the modelling salons at seventeen. That decision was the reason why she'd managed to develop what had turned out to be an exceptionally good mind.

But there was an obstinate air of decision on that full mouth which had almost persuaded Mrs Prenderghast not to take Lola on during the first interview. Mrs Prenderghast set great store by uncontroversiality in her companions. Mrs Prenderghast also preferred her companions to be plain—which Lola definitely wasn't. And she didn't want some honeypot who would bring men buzzing round night and day. But she had sensed something else about Lola—a quiet discipline which held that considerable beauty in check.

Hearing that she was taking a job as a lady's companion had greatly amused Tom, Lola remembered wryly. With her mother's misty green eyes, she'd also inherited a sparkling, deeply feminine temperament that could be almost explosively passionate when stirred. Lola adored laughter and couldn't hold back tears. Her mobile emotions surfaced with an ease that had always made her a helpless victim to her father's or Tom's teasing. She rose to the bait ridiculously quickly, and until very recently, either of them had been able to ignite her to a shimmering tempest of indignation—a display which her father had once admiringly compared to the aurora borealis.

It was really quite astonishing that she hadn't already fallen head-over-heels in love at least a dozen times. Anyone who managed to stir those female emotions of hers ought to have a quite remarkable reaction on hand! Somehow, though, no one had managed. 'It's like harnessing the sea to make electricity,' a rueful boyfriend had once commented. 'The idea is fabulous, but the practicalities are proving remarkably hard to master. . .'

'Don't forget my medicines, sweetie,' Mrs Prenderghast called.

'I won't,' she promised.

And winced at the dull note in her own voice.

Those hard-to-control emotions of hers were very subdued lately, Lola thought tiredly. 'Yes, Mrs Prenderghast' and 'No, Mrs Prenderghast' were about all she seemed able to manage. Her capacity for laughter and delight seemed to have tarnished over the past months, as though the keen edge of her spirit itself were being dulled. Maybe the after-effects of her mother's death were still slamming home, somewhere deep inside her heart?

The Golightly family had been loving, warm, tightly knit. Lola still found herself stunned at the way the winds of fate had scattered them all so suddenly and ruthlessly. Tom in Japan, studying hi-fi technology with Hitachi, her father promoted to chairman of the board, now working in a glass tower in London. And her mother, the most vital, joyful person she'd ever known, dead.

Hospitalised for a minor gynaecological operation two years ago, Zara Golightly had been given a normally harmless drug to sedate her. The 5cc of straw-coloured fluid had caused the tiny platelets in her blood to adhere disastrously, and the resulting embolism had taken her life as instantaneously as a pistol-shot. A one-in-a-million reaction, the doctors had called it. Which hadn't lessened the unbearable pain of her loss to her husband and two children.

Lola buttoned on a cool white frock and blouse, her eyes dark with the sad memories. Lola Golightly, BA. That was another irony; the recession, high unemployment, and cut-backs in education had all but obliterated her job prospects. She'd graduated in the summer, and had abruptly found herself alone in her tiny digs in London at the age of twenty-two, with a degree in Renaissance Studies, and no chance at all of getting the lecturing job she'd set her heart on when she'd embarked on her studies. Tom and her father had badly wanted her to go and live with one or the other of them; and her father had offered as much financial help as she needed. But Lola had known that she was going to have to make her own life somehow, even if that meant setting her sights rather lower than she'd intended. And that had meant taking jobs like this one until an opening in some school or university showed itself.

'Lola,' Mrs Prenderghast shouted, 'My dressing-gown, sweetie.'

Lola sighed again as she carried the garish swathe of silk through to the bathroom. It wasn't always easy waiting hand and foot on someone like Mamie, especially when you'd spent the past three years studying Michelangelo and Leonardo da Vinci. But the discipline, she told herself, was undoubtedly doing her immortal soul a power of good.

'Feeling cooler?' she smiled as Mrs Prenderghast slid her plump arms into the gown.

'Much.' She waddled past Lola. 'In fact, I feel well enough to deal with Armand right now. Fix me another daiquiri, will you, dear?'

As she measured the free-with-the-suite rum into the long glass, Lola wondered ironically whether the Hotel Grande management had any idea of the quantities of Bacardi and lime Mrs Prenderghast could go through in ten days. Some writers, she'd heard, sharpened pencils or neatened their desks before writing. Mrs Prenderghast drank three daiquiris.

The discreet clatter of the electronic typewriter rose from the balcony as she made the drink. That was how Viola May Banksteads wrote; her lurid imagination floated on a mild alcoholic haze.

Taking the already dewy glass through to her employer, Lola had a sudden pang of compassion for Mrs Prenderghast. For all her success and wealth, she was a slightly pathetic person. A grotesque, garish old woman tanking herself up on rum to stimulate her garish schoolgirl fantasies.

'Here,' she said gently, putting the glass down. 'I haven't made it too strong. You know what the doctor in Milan said about alcohol and hot weather.'

Mrs Prenderghast nodded impatiently, and gulped at the drink.

The page she was working on, Lola saw over her shoulder, started:

'Armand crushed her mouth to his with

*savage lust, his teeth drawing blood from her
tortured lips, then thrust her contemptuously
back on to the bed. "I'll be back tonight," he
sneered, "to ravish that pale body once again!"
And with a Satanic guffaw, he vaulted ath-
letically into the Rolls-Royce coupé. Laetitia
sobbed helplessly, the cruel chains biting into
her frail wrists.'*

Lola bit back a smile. Viola May was on top
money-spinning form.

'I'm just going downstairs for a few minutes,'
she told her employer. Mrs Prenderghast nodded
again, and Lola went back to her bedroom to slip
low-heeled sandals on.

In the opulent hotel shops downstairs, Lola
booked an appointment for Mrs Prenderghast at
the hairdressing salon, bought herself some
English magazines and a guide to Nice, was
tempted by some beautiful but far too costly silk
scarves, and then paused dreamily in front of the
small and dazzling Cartier display. No doubt Mrs
Prenderghast would spend an hour or two here;
she bought herself diamonds in the careless way
ordinary women bought cosmetics, and she was
travelling with a quantity of jewellery which had
been giving Lola nightmares. How they'd managed
to avoid leaving behind them a bracelet or two
lying in basins or on coffee-tables, she'd never
know.

The lifestyle was nothing if not stylish!
Tomorrow was set aside for a junket with Mrs
Prenderghast's French publishers aboard some
glamorous local playboy's sixty-foot schooner, and
the next day they were due at the Baroness Var's
summer villa. . .

'Excuse me—Mam'selle——'

She turned to face two small, wispy, and unmistakably English ladies in their late fifties or early sixties.

'Yes?' she smiled.

'So sorry to intrude,' said the one who had spoken, 'but we couldn't help noticing—the lady you came through the foyer with earlier on—was that by *any* chance Viola May Banksteads?'

'Yes, it was,' Lola nodded.

'We thought so,' the other lady breathed happily. 'We saw her picture in *Woman's Own* once, and we were sure it must be her. We read *all* her books. We think she's wonderful!'

'Do you think,' the younger sister pleaded, producing a book from her handbag, 'could she possibly find time to autograph this——?'

It was a copy of *Passion's Slave*, one of Mrs Prenderghast's top sellers. The lurid cover, depicting a typical Banksteads' rape-scene, was oddly incongruous in the wispy lady's hands.

'Of course,' Lola promised gently, taking the book. 'Mrs Pre——' Just in time she remembered that Mrs Prenderghast didn't like her real name to be known. '—er, Miss Banksteads will be delighted to find two such devoted admirers here in Nice.'

'The Misses Jenkins,' the older sister beamed. 'Charlotte—that's my sister—and Cynthia.'

'Pleased to meet you,' Lola said, shaking the thin, white-kid-gloved hands one after another. 'I'm Lola Golightly, Miss Banksteads' travelling companion.'

'Pleased to meet *you*. And is Miss Banksteads here gathering material for another book, Miss Golightly?' the younger sister asked eagerly.

'Yes, she's busy with her latest book right now.

Miss Banksteads spends three months of the year abroad, getting inspiration for her novels.' She gave them a brief itinerary of their tour so far.

'And you've travelled with her all the way?' Cynthia Jenkins asked, wide-eyed. Lola nodded. She could see the Jenkinses thinking what a fabulous time she must have had.

Somehow, though, she didn't have any vivid memories of Colisseums or Alps or Black Forests. All she seemed to be able to recall were three relentless months of Mrs Prenderghast!

'How lucky you are,' Charlotte Jenkins sighed dreamily, 'to see all those places, *and* have the privilege of working for Miss Banksteads.'

'It's a great honour,' Lola nodded solemnly. She put the book in her own bag. 'I'll ask Miss Banksteads to autograph this, and then I'll leave it at the reception-desk for you. Will that be all right?'

'Perfectly all right,' beamed Cynthia Jenkins. Lola said goodbye to the English exiles, and watched them scurry out of the shopping mall. Then she set off towards the lift.

Her mood of peaceful reverie was shattered instantly as she opened the highly varnished door of Suite 225.

'... and *you*, you ugly baboon, are an ill-mannered lout!'

The piercing voice, unquestionably Mrs Prenderghast's, came from the balcony. As she ran to the rescue, Lola could hear a gruff, foreign, male voice answering angrily.

Mrs Prenderghast was standing by her typewriter, arms akimbo and beaky face mottled with indignation. There was a partition of lush plants separating their balcony from the next one, and over the dieffenbachias and dracaenias the rocky head of the Bulgarian gentleman was protruding. He was looking even angrier than Mrs Prenderghast.

'I did not come here to listen to a secretary,' he was snarling, 'I must hov slip! It is imperative! Silence pliss!'

'Silence yourself, you—you Bulgarian monster,' Mrs Prenderghast shot back, enraged at being called a secretary. She shook a diamond-studded fist at their neighbour. 'I shall complain to the manager about you!'

Gritting her teeth, Lola girded her loins for the fray, and emerged on to the balcony with her professional smile in place. 'Can I help?' she asked soothingly.

'I shall complain myself,' the Bulgarian monster said furiously, shaking his own boulder-like fist in return. *'Vache Anglaise!'*

'What on earth is going on?' Lola asked, half-anticipating that the Bulgarian might actually clamber over the partition and hurl Mrs Prenderghast off the balcony, twenty-two stories down.

'This cave-man,' Mrs Prenderghast spat out, gesturing at her opponent, 'has the effrontery to want me to stop typing!'

'Yes,' the Bulgarian nodded, purple-faced. 'Stop! Stop! This is too much! It is intolerable! *Je suis très fatigué.*' He pantomimed sleep for a second, then glared at them. 'I am trying to slip,' he roared. 'It is *impossible* to slip with your infernal tac-tac tac-tac tac-tac!'

'I think we'd better go inside,' Lola suggested, smiling brightly at the Bulgarian.

'I'm damned if I will!' Mrs Prenderghast

snapped. 'This isn't Bulgaria, d'you hear, it's France!'

'Tac-tac tac-tac tac-tac,' the Bulgarian rattled again, venomously mimicking the typewriter. 'Hov you no consideration for other pipple? You must stop!'

'She's stopping right now,' Lola assured him placatingly, and gave him another beam as she put her shoulder to her employer's bulk. Her three creative daiquiris had made Mrs Prenderghast unusually combative. It was tempting to just hand them each a hatchet and tell them to get on with it—but the Bulgarian might well remove her source of employment, permanently. Lola heaved the writer unceremoniously through the French door, and slammed it behind them. The Bulgarian could still be heard shouting abuse over the partition. Lola's temper, frayed by the various contretemps of the day, stretched dangerously.

She stalked out on to the balcony again, and looked the Bulgarian squarely in the eye.

'You've made your point,' she told him shortly. 'She's stopped now.' The Bulgarian's mouth, open in mid-curse, snapped shut under the influence of Lola's cool gaze. He disappeared, like Mr Punch, vertically downwards.

'I'm going to complain to the manager this instant!' Mrs Prenderghast quivered as Lola came back inside. 'The man was positively abusive!'

'I wouldn't bother,' Lola soothed. 'I think he just likes to sleep in the afternoon, and the noise of the typewriter was keeping him awake.'

'But I've got my book to write! I can't stop typing every time some damned Bulgar wants to sleep in the afternoon!'

'I'll get your typewriter back inside in a minute,' Lola promised, piloting Mrs Prenderghast towards the cocktail cabinet. 'He won't be able to hear you if you type indoors—and if you use the table next to the balcony you'll still have the sea-view. I'll make you another daiquiri, shall I?'

'Damned foreigners,' Mrs Prenderghast rumbled. But it was the rumble of a subsiding volcano. Lola put just two drops of rum into the lime-juice, knowing that Mrs Prenderghast probably wouldn't know the difference by now.

'First he steals our suite,' Mrs Prenderghast rumbled on, gulping at the drink, 'then he has the cheek to complain about my typing. There's too much rum in this daiquiri, Lola. No, no, don't touch it. I'll drink it as it is.'

Lola staggered back inside with the typewriter, put it on the table next to the window, fetched the rest of the manuscript, and closed the balcony door.

'There,' she smiled. 'It was getting chilly outside, anyway.'

'Oh well.' Grumpily, the writer settled down in her new position. She gave Lola a grudging half-smile. 'I've never known anyone like you for being able to smooth things over,' she conceded. 'What would I do without you?'

'All part of the service.'

Lola watched her warily for a while, nevertheless, as she got down to work again; then, feeling that hostilities had been suspended, went through to the bathroom to unpack Mrs Prenderghast's medicine-bag. It contained a formidable array of painkillers, sleeping-tablets, laxatives, emetics, eye-lotions, insect-bite creams, antacids, nose-drops, smelling-salts and several dozen other bottles and tubes that Lola could only guess at. Her employer was addicted to patent medicines. She filled the bathroom cabinet like a miniature pharmacy, knowing that Mrs Prenderghast wouldn't feel at home until her medicines were all laid out.

Then, feeling exhausted, she retired to her own bedroom, and curled up on the plush bed with a magazine. It was turning out to be another perfect day. An hour and a half to dinner. Four hours to bed-time. Twenty-eight days to the end of this holiday.

She buried herself in the article on stress relief.

Lola stirred into wakefulness for the third time that night. The five-course dinner had been delicious, but far too rich. At midnight she'd heard the sound of Mrs Prenderghast mixing herself a glass of bicarbonate, followed by a sonorous belch. She herself had been feeling uncomfortable, and the past couple of hours' sleep had been restless. She reached for her alarm-clock in the gloom. It was two-thirty a.m. She rolled over, feeling hot, and kicked the blankets off.

Then she heard it again. The noise that had awoken her. It was a small scratching sound from the next room. Lola scrunched her face into the pillow resentfully. She didn't feel like getting up to investigate, and maybe confronting a French mouse, or something worse. Maybe it would just go away.

Conscience pricked at her. She was, after all, more or less responsible for Mrs Prenderghast, and the mouse, after all, might be gnawing at *Unquenchable Flame of the Heart*. Feeling grumpy, she swung her long legs out of bed, and wearing her flimsy nightgown, padded through into the drawing-room, pulling her thick hair into some semblance of order.

The moonlit room was peaceful. Mrs Prenderghast's diamonds glittered in an untidy heap on the coffee-table. The manuscript was neatly piled next to the typewriter. There was no obvious source for the noise, and Lola turned to go back to bed, yawning.

Then froze in her tracks. A shadow had fallen over one of the windows, where no shadow could possibly fall, twenty-two stories up in the air. With a stealthy creak, it swung open. A silent scream swelled in Lola's throat as she shrank back against the wall and watched with terrified eyes.

Like a shadow detached from the night itself, a man swung himself lithely through the open window, and dropped silently on to the carpet. He was tall, wearing tight black jeans and a black polo-neck which clung to the taut lines of his panther-lean body. A black velvet carnival mask hugged his cheekbones.

Working with quiet, deadly efficiency, he unclipped the nylon mountaineer's cord that was attached to the thick leather belt round his waist, and looped it round the window-catch. Then he turned, drawing a pencil-thin torch from the flat packed strapped to his hip.

Lola was petrified, unable to breathe or stir. Part of the horror was the sheer impossibility of his being there at all. Where in God's name had he come from, well over three hundred feet up? He was the most frightening presence she had ever seen, moving with the silent, efficient grace of some feral creature. The black mask made him as grim as death itself.

The thin, bright beam stabbed across the room,

then paused on the glittering heap of diamonds on the coffee-table. She couldn't help it. A tiny noise escaped her lips. The blade of light whipped up to her eyes, dazzling her, and she dragged in her breath to scream.

CHAPTER TWO

HE sprang at her before a sound could escape her lips, and spun her round, his hand clamping hard over her mouth as he pinioned her against his chest.

Lola struggled frantically, her lungs bursting, but he was far too strong. Tall as she was, he was taller, and his body had the ruthless speed of an athlete's. He kicked her legs out from under her, lowering her silently to an ungainly sitting position against the wall, then crouched over her, his hand still clamped over her lips. She stared up into the masked face with the paralysed terror of a bird confronting a cobra.

A pair of eyes as golden as any mountain-lion's surveyed her calmly through the slits in the black velvet. All she could see of his face was his mouth, which was ruthlessly male, and a chiselled jawline.

'Chut, Mademoiselle,' he whispered. She was desperate for oxygen, and as his fingers released her mouth, she let the pent-up air out in a gasp. He laid a warning finger against her lips. 'Tais-toi.' He played the pen-light quickly across her face, and down over her long, tanned legs, exposed almost to the hips by her position.

She hauled the silk down furiously, trying to squirm upright.

'Who are you?' she demanded in an unsteady hiss, horribly aware of the possibility that he might slit her throat there and then. The dark pupils in the golden eyes widened for a second.

28

'You are English.' Her hair had tumbled over her face in the struggle, and he brushed it out of her eyes, studying her more carefully. A slow smile curved into place. 'And what are you doing up so late, Mam'selle?'

'I heard a noise.' She was beginning to shake as reaction to the shock began to set in. 'What the hell are *you* doing here?'

'Breaking and entering. Naturally.' His smile disturbed her suddenly; there was a cruel hint to the curve of his full lower lip. 'Why else would I go to all this trouble? Now—where is your friend?'

'If you try and hurt Mrs Prenderghast,' Lola threatened in a quavering whisper, 'I'll scratch your eyes out. She's only an old woman. All her diamonds are over there——'

'Ah.' He stared at her for a motionless second, then glanced thoughtfully at the sparkling pile on the table. 'Don't worry—your Mrs Prenderghast is quite safe.' His voice was faintly accented, and had a lingering, velvety warmth in its deep tones. She could smell some expensive, aromatic after-shave on him, and it occurred to her that he was a very civilised burglar. If he let her go, even for a second, she was going to scream her head off—or bounce an ashtray off *his*.

His eyes were really extraordinary. They were lambent, with a fierce golden flame in their depths, compelling and dangerous. The jet-black pupils probed her own for a few more seconds, and she was deeply relieved when he stood up, and walked over to the table, scooping up the gems. He studied them with the same thoughtful air.

Lola rose rather unsteadily to her own feet, wishing to heaven that she was wearing something more substantial than the transparent and girlishly short chemise that was her usual summer nightwear. She felt extremely vulnerable facing her first burglar like this.

'Worth about ten thousand pounds?' he suggested, tossing the gems in his hand. She nodded, trying to estimate the distance between her and the telephone. His tiger's eyes dropped to study her figure with calm appreciation. The dark centres of her breasts were visible against the pearly material. She folded her arms hurriedly, feeling naked and angry.

'Those are the most valuable things in the flat,' she assured him in a low voice.

'Indeed?' That same mocking smile carved shadows at the corners of a mouth handsome enough to belong to the devil himself. He seemed to be hesitating. 'Unfortunately, Mam'selle, I am looking for something of infinitely more value.' He considered her pale, alarmed face for a second. 'If I swear I do not intend to harm either you or your employer, can I trust you to hold your tongue?'

Lola nodded vigorously, crossing her mental fingers like mad. He dropped the diamonds casually back on to the table, and walked swiftly across towards the balcony.

The manuscript! It came to her in a flash. Diamonds were traceable—but an ingenious crook could ransom a nearly completed Banksteads manuscript for hundreds of thousands! And as he reached out, Lola siezed her chance.

She clenched her fists, shut her eyes, and screamed as loudly and as piercingly as she could.

The man in black spun round in a crouch. She kept screaming, fear adding power to her lungs, *'Help! Police! Help!!!'* He strode swiftly over to her, and she snatched up a nearby vase, determined to sell her life dearly. Unbelievably, though, there was a wry smile on his face.

'I thought I could trust you,' he reproved gently. 'But at least you have spirit.' Distant shouts could be heard from along the corridor. Ignoring her poised vase, he pulled her swiftly towards him, and kissed her hard on the lips. *'A bientôt,'* he murmured, staring into her eyes. 'Some other time, perhaps.'

She stood frozen, the memory of his lips warm on hers as he ran to the window, and slotted the steel clip on to his belt. He didn't look back as he hauled himself through the frame. Lola found herself biting her knuckles in horror at the prospect of her first and only real live cat-burglar plummeting over twenty stories down; but with a mountain-climber's effortless skill, he kicked away from the wall, and swung on the nylon cord out of sight.

Just as he did so, Mrs Prenderghast billowed into the room in a tropical-print *peignoir*, and switched on the light.

'God in Heaven, girl!' Sleep had made her eyes puffy, and she glared at Lola blearily. 'You nearly gave me a heart-attack! What on earth is going on?'

'A burglar——' Lola gasped, still stunned by what had happened. 'There!'

'What burglar?' Mrs Prenderghast demanded scornfully. The door of the suite burst open, and the bald manager rushed in, skeleton key in one hand and a pistol in the other. In his wake was a female member of the hotel's staff, and the Bulgarian monster, resplendent in a crimson dressing-gown. The manager stopped short at the sight of Lola with her vase still clutched in one hand.

'Madame,' he said dramatically, addressing Mrs Prenderghast, 'are you all right?'

'Of course I'm all right,' she snapped in reply. She pointed accusingly at Lola. 'She says she saw a burglar.'

'A burglar? *Un cambrioleur?*'

'A cat-burglar. He—he came through that window,' Lola stammered, pointing.

The Bulgarian's black eyes widened in alarm.

'*Un cambrioleur?*' he grunted, and scurried rapidly back to his own suite. More guests were materialising in the doorway, fastening dressing-gowns and staring silently in.

The manager trotted over to the window, and peered cautiously out, the pistol clutched in his hand.

Lola held her breath, but the manager's bald head swivelled up and down uneventfully, and he turned to face them with a shrug.

'Nothing.'

'It's unlike you to behave so stupidly, Lola,' Mrs Prenderghast snapped.

'I *saw* him,' Lola insisted, running to the window to check for herself. The sheer walls of the hotel were bare in the moonlight. And it was a very long way down. Where the hell had he got to? Feeling cold inside, she withdrew her head to meet several pairs of accusing eyes. 'He was there,' she protested helplessly, her voice rising. 'I swear he was! All in black, with a nylon rope——' Briefly, she told them the bare bones of what had happened. Their faces were blank, and she guessed with a stab of frustration that they'd all be thinking *hysteria*.

'So,' the manager said, trying not to show that he was humouring her, 'you heard a noise. You had had indigestion.' She nodded impatiently. 'You got up out of your bed. When you came in here, the *cambrioleur* was waiting, dressed all in black. You screamed. You picked up the vase.' Lola looked at the thing, still in her hand. It was wafer-thin porcelain, and it would have been about as effective as a toothpick. She put it down, feeling an idiot. 'Whereupon he—er—kissed you. And then he vanished, leaving no trace. Yes?'

'Yes,' she insisted, beginning to feel indignant. 'That's exactly what took place!'

'My diamonds are still all here,' Mrs Prenderghast pointed out disbelievingly, poking at the sparkly heap with a red-nailed claw. Everyone looked at Lola again.

'He picked them up,' she told them impatiently, running her hand through her untidy hair in an unconscious echo of the burglar's caress, 'and then he just put them down again. He didn't seem to want them!'

'With your permission, Madame.' The manager tucked his gun back into his pocket, and picked up the telephone. He spoke rapidly in French to someone on the other end, and replaced the receiver after a succession of brisk nods. 'The hotel detectives have seen nothing tonight,' he said. 'No one has come in or out, up or down. And they are very vigilant, I assure you.'

'But I *spoke* to him,' Lola insisted desperately, feeling that this was turning into some kind of bad dream. 'He didn't take anything, but only because I started screaming. I think he was after Mrs Prenderghast's novel.' She drew a deep breath. 'I *know* he was here. He—he kissed me!'

There was a ripple of laughter, and she flushed scarlet. Realising suddenly that her nightgown was probably completely transparent in the light, she edged quickly behind a sofa, furious at their incredulity. They must all think her mad!

'It is completely impossible for anyone to get into these suites, Mam'selle,' the manager said gently. His smile was sympathetic. 'You can see that for yourself. Not even an expert mountaineer could climb up the walls. Perhaps the animal in question was not a cat, but a nightmare. Is it not possible that you had a bad dream——?'

'I swear I saw him,' Lola repeated helplessly. She went back to the window, and peered out. The Mediterranean night was so still that she could even hear the distant whisper of the sea. 'I wasn't dreaming!'

'You had too much lobster for dinner,' Mrs Prenderghast said acidly. Her cheeks wobbled with indignation. 'I've never *known* you be so flighty. Fancy waking the entire hotel like this!'

Lola could only shake her head silently. The fact that he had vanished into the night didn't mean he had been any kind of hallucination. She could still feel his warmth on her mouth! And suppose he came back?

'*Alors,*' the manager said patiently, as though reading her thoughts, 'I shall instruct the detectives to be especially vigilant from now on.' He went to the open window, and slammed it firmly shut, locking it. 'And someone will stand guard outside the door tonight, just in case——'

'Fiddlesticks,' Mrs Prenderghast snorted, 'I don't want to be harassed with a lot of clumsy ex-policemen. All I want is a bit of *privacy!*'

Her glare was awesome. The other guests began shuffling away to their rooms, some muttering indignantly at having been disturbed for nothing, but many with open grins on their faces. The chambermaid, too, retired discreetly.

Lola pressed her fists tiredly into her eyes. The stranger who had kissed her five minutes ago had made her look the biggest fool in France tonight. And he was out there in the darkness somewhere, she knew it, those fire-gold eyes laughing. Damn him! She sighed. At least she had saved *Unquenchable Flame of the Heart* from kidnap, of that she was utterly convinced.

'You've made us the laughing-stock of the whole place,' Mrs Prenderghast accused. There was no trace of gratitude in her expression.

'*Mais non,* Madame,' the manager said mildly, 'Mam'selle was frightened. She had a vivid dream. Such things are not uncommon when one comes to a strange place for the first time—and the lobster Thermidor was a *little* rich.' He smiled cautiously. 'I would advise Madame, however, to leave her diamonds in the hotel safe——'

'I don't want your opinion, thank you,' Mrs Prenderghast rapped. Her earlier hostility to the man had been redoubled, it seemed, by the feeling that she had been made to look ridiculous in front of him. 'My companion simply had a bad dream. And now I'd be grateful for a little privacy!'

The manager ushered himself out hastily, closing the door as he went.

'Bursting into people's apartments,' Mrs Prenderghast snarled at the gleaming door. 'If only de Gaulle were alive——' She turned indignantly to Lola, who was sitting wearily on the arm of a sofa. 'And what have *you* got to say for yourself?'

'I saw him,' Lola repeated quietly. It was infuriating to be disbelieved, no matter how slender the evidence, and it was extremely humiliating to be accused of eating too much lobster and dreaming up burglars, and her temper was beginning to fray. She kept her voice level. 'It wasn't a dream. I saw him, and spoke to him, and——'

'And kissed him,' Mrs Prenderghast concluded. 'No doubt! To think I thought you were so reliable! You'd better not eat any more lobster while we're here, that's a certainty.' She snatched up her diamonds and glared at Lola. 'And now we shall have everybody in the hotel staring at us and whispering for days.' She stalked to the bathroom, and returned with one of her dozens of medicine bottles. 'There,' she said imperiously, thrusting it at Lola. '*That* may subdue your imagination!'

Milk of Magnesia.

From behind her slammed door, Lola could hear her rasping, '*And* I shall have to take two more sleeping-pills. . . .'

Peace descended once again upon the Hotel Grande. The perfect end to a perfect day. Trying to control her anger, Lola placed the Magnesia bottle carefully on the coffee-table, heaved herself up, and walked slowly back to bed.

It was three-fifteen.

She curled up in a resentful, smouldering ball, knowing that sleep was practically impossible. Why hadn't they believed her, the idiots? Because it was much too alarming to believe that a man could climb up to a twenty-second storey window, and walk in as casually as if on to a yacht, that was why!

The memory of a beautiful male mouth haunted her dreams maddeningly.

The MY *Casablanca*, the schooner on which they

were to spend the afternoon, was a blaze of white paintwork and polished brass against the vivid blue crescent of the harbour.

'And *Scarlet Destiny* has been doing particularly well for the past six months,' Vivien Roche assured Mrs Prenderghast as they walked down to the pier. 'The French title, as I'm sure you know, is *Scandale*. Catchy, no? Top of the hardcover bestsellers for five weeks, which is very good going for a book in translation——'

Mrs Prenderghast hadn't been cut out by Nature as a listener, but since Mme Roche's main subject had been the huge success of Viola May Banksteads in France, Mrs Prenderghast had been beaming contentedly all morning. Lola had been amused to find that Viola May's French pen-name was Jacqueline Lalique. The name had screamed at her from the vivid covers of the twenty thousand copies of *Scandale* that Mme Roche had proudly shown them in the publisher's store-rooms, waiting for distribution.

She walked with the two women to the long white yacht, soaking up the sun and the beauty of her surroundings. There had been dozens of meetings like this on the holiday, with publishers, editors and agents in half the major cities of Europe. Mrs Prenderghast was very big business indeed, and people had given her the kind of reception normally accorded to film stars or politicians. It had sometimes made Lola smile faintly to see Mrs Prenderghast's garishly outfitted, lumpy figure waddling along so incongruously at the centre of so much elegant and fashionable attention. Lola herself was wearing a muted green trouser-suit with a lacy white blouse, the sort of gently classical clothing that she felt wouldn't make her too conspicuous at her employer's side. She'd tied her dark-gold hair back in a spinsterish bun, but despite her minimal make-up, she was a radiantly beautiful young woman as she followed Mrs Prenderghast and Mme Roche up the gangplank to where a crowd of people were waiting to greet them on deck.

There were several introductions to be made. A small but select party of people, mostly connected with the publishing trade, had assembled on the yacht to meet Mrs Prenderghast. Lola smiled and murmured through the introductions, not bothering to try and remember any of the names that went with the prosperous faces. She didn't count here, and never would; and it wasn't likely any of these people would be interested in discussing the Renaissance in France.

'My companion, Lola Golightly,' Mrs Prenderghast said as Lola shook hands with the last of the guests, an elderly journalist who specialised in literary reviews.

'What a *fascinating* name!' the critic smiled as he bowed. 'And a fascinating face. I compliment you on your choice of companion, Madame!'

Lola smiled noncommittally. His fascination would probably wane once he discovered her lowly role in the hierarchy!

'And now,' Mme Roche said, guiding them through the crowd, her dark face flushed with excitement, 'I want you to meet someone very special indeed—our host for this afternoon, César Levertov. César, this is Mrs Prenderghast, and her companion, Lola Golightly.'

César Levertov was easily the tallest man on the yacht.

He was also quite the most striking man Lola

had ever seen. She was instantly conscious of a raw masculine presence that wasn't even slightly muted by the immaculate white slacks and the cream blazer with the gilt badge of some exclusive club on the pocket. His face was dark, ultra-masculine, and alight with vivid, wicked life. The sexuality of a frankly beautiful mouth was almost contradicted by harsh lines of cheekbones and jaw, and a fiercely aquiline nose that seemed to hint at cruelty; and his crisp black hair was brushed carelessly back around neat ears and a distinguished brow. There were dramatic silver glints at his temples, and he looked an athletic and magnificently fit thirty-five.

He bowed slightly as he took Mrs Prenderghast's diamond-studded claw.

'Delighted to meet you, Madame,' he said gently.

'Delighted to meet *you*,' Mrs Prenderghast gushed, her plump cheeks pinkening as she ogled up at him. 'It's so very kind of you to invite us all aboard your *exquisite* yacht, Monsieur Levertov——'

'Oh, please—César.' He moved with a kind of instinctive animal grace that was quintessentially, disturbingly, male. As he turned to Lola, wicked beauty glinting in his smile, his eyes flared gold at her.

'And this is your charming companion—Lola?'

Lola didn't say anything.

She was frozen, her mouth open. *The cat-burglar*. There wasn't the slightest shred of doubt in her mind that he knew she had recognised him. Who wouldn't recognise those unforgettable eyes and that heart-stopping smile? She even caught a tantalising hint of that aromatic, expensive-smelling aftershave on his tanned skin.

He took her hand, and bowed over it, then straightened to laugh mockingly into her face.

Not open laughter—a sparkling, silent amusement that dared her to even breathe a word of what she knew.

Crimson-cheeked, she pulled her hand out of his, glaring back at him. Yes, it was her midnight panther all right. Despite the velvet mask, no woman could ever have forgotten the supremely confident, arrogant way that body moved, or the mocking laughter in that passionate mouth, with its bittersweet downward curve.

He dropped his gaze to Lola's full mouth, then to a cool appraisal of her figure.

'Have we not met before, Lola?' he asked gravely, mischief igniting in his eyes as they met hers again. As she gaped like a goldfish for an answer to such a stunningly impertinent question, Mrs Prenderghast cut in, 'I'm sure that's impossible, César. Lola's only just finished a university degree in England.' She patted Lola's arm condescendingly. 'I'm showing her a little of the world while she makes her mind up about her next job.'

'Ah.' Gravely, César Levertov turned his extraordinary golden gaze back to the older woman. 'It must have been in some other incarnation, then. It seems that you are indeed Lola's benefactress, Mrs Prenderghast.'

'Call me Mamie.' Mrs Prenderghast straightened her yellow and turquoise dress with a little wiggle, and rolled her eyes up at him. 'I think your yacht is simply too beautiful for words, César.'

'Indeed?' he purred. He offered an arm to Mrs Prenderghast with the grace of centuries of breeding. 'Then you must allow me to show you around. Perhaps you will accompany me to the bridge while we sail out of the harbour?' He bowed to Lola and the publisher. 'With your permission, *Mesdames*.'

'*Charming* man,' Mme Roche whispered in Lola's ear as he led the celebrated author, positively gliding on her scarlet high-heels, towards the bridge.

'Charming,' Lola said through clenched teeth. She was still feeling totally flabbergasted. What in God's name could she do? Denounce César Levertov as a thief? She could just imagine the expressions on all the well-bred, well-fed faces around her. She shook her head slowly, watching the tall, elegant figure in disbelief.

'A man of considerable culture,' Mme Roche went on admiringly. She cocked her dark head on one side, bird-like. 'He has so many interests in so many different fields.'

'I'll bet,' Lola said acidly, her poise beginning to return. She glanced around the beautiful schooner. What weird impulse would drive a man like this— aristocratic, privileged, wealthy—to risk his life and reputation swinging himself into high-rise hotel suites in the dead of night? Boredom? Or maybe he actually financed all this luxury by stealing diamonds and manuscripts from the best hotels in Nice? 'What fields, exactly?' she asked Mme Roche.

'Publishing, naturally. And I believe he owns an aircraft design company.' The publisher shrugged. 'One does not enquire too deeply, of course.'

'Of course,' Lola said with a hint of irony.

'César is part-Russian, you know,' Mme Roche went on. 'His grandfather escaped to France during the Revolution, in 1917, at the age of nineteen. A prince, one of the great Levertov family, Is that not romantic?'

'Very.'

'He married into the Gabriel family, Counts of Calvados-Eure. But César still keeps the Levertov name.' The motors of the great yacht had been throbbing under their feet, and the two dozen or so guests broke into a festive cheer as the *Casablanca* turned slowly to the mouth of the harbour, and began her stately way out to sea.

'Count César Levertov,' Lola murmured softly. It would be amusing to ruffle that supremely male calm! What would happen if she simply came out with an accusation?

Mme Roche peered at her curiously. '*Have* you met him before, Miss Golightly?'

'What——? Oh. No, I'm afraid Monsieur Levertov was mistaken,' she smiled. But she was thinking of that whispered 'Some other time, perhaps' last night. He must have known he would meet her again today. Really, the barefaced cheek of the man was superb! She felt her anger begin to subside as she got over the shock of seeing her cat-burglar again. Perhaps the day on the schooner was not going to be as dull an occasion as she'd anticipated!

In fact, it was a glorious day. Once beyond the confines of the harbour, the air became fresh and tangy, and the sun baked down blissfully. The crew had prepared a buffet on the main deck, and conversation centred around it for a couple of hours. Mrs Prenderghast, of course, held court like some Hollywood *diva*, and Lola was vaguely irritated, though she didn't want to be, to see that César Levertov paid her the most flattering attention, nodding gravely at all her inane pronouncements as though she were an oracle of wisdom. A heady kind of flattery. Lola guessed by Mrs Prenderghast's pinkness and beaming smiles that the writer was imagining herself twenty and fascinating again.

Mingling with her irritation, though, was Lola's perplexity about the man himself. Moving at the fringes of the party, trying to avoid various flirtatious males, none of whom seemed to be under fifty, she wondered what on earth to do with the rather dangerous knowledge she alone had about César Levertov. Was it the sort of thing one could possibly go to the police with? He was obviously highly respected—even adored—around Nice. How could she hope to assail that reputation with a dubious claim to have recognised those amber-- flecked golden eyes one frightened midnight?

It also occurred to her that a man as athletic and ruthless as César Levertov would find it very easy to dispose of a troublesome witness.

Maybe even in the midst of a party on a sunny Mediterranean afternoon.

Lola stared down at the ultramarine water below, and felt suddenly cold. Knowing a powerful man's secrets was a chilly kind of thrill. Maybe it wouldn't be so amusing to accuse him, after all!

Lola leaned against the rail, and glanced across at Mrs Prenderghast, now deep in discussions about the sales of her books in Europe. The old woman was like some ugly Baroque fountain, pouring out money and surrounded by people eager to dip their handkerchiefs and pails in the bonanza. Maybe they would erect a statue to her one day, she thought with an inner grin. Holding a spouting pen aloft.

'Care to share the joke?'

Lola almost choked into her champagne as César Levertov materialised beside her, taking her arm firmly in his hand. 'You should be mingling,' he commanded, piloting her towards a group of people nearby. Still mentally off-balance, she forced smiles through the various introductions he made.

'You're Mamie's companion, aren't you?' a moustached man asked in a heavy French accent. 'Apparently you're an expert on the Renaissance in Europe?'

'She has been greater things than that,' César interrupted before Lola could answer. 'Miss Golightly and I,' he informed them gravely, 'have met once before—in a previous incarnation.' There were smiles all round, and Lola kept her expression studiously neutral, though she could feel her cheeks reddening. That mocking smile would disappear fast if she revealed where they really *had* met!

'And where was that, pray?' she asked coolly.

'You were Cleopatra,' he informed her, 'and I was a humble Egyptian slave.'

'I hope I had you beheaded,' she retorted drily, not in the mood for this kind of flirtatious teasing.

'Indeed you did.' The golden eyes mocked her. 'But I got my revenge several centuries later— when I was Robespierre, and you were Marie Antoinette.'

'A bloodthirsty relationship,' one of the women smiled. 'I wonder what you're going to be to each other in this life?'

'Perhaps I'll turn Portia,' Lola suggested tartly, 'and have you imprisoned.' His ironic smile only widened.

'On what charge?'

'I could think of something,' she threatened, meeting his stare levelly. 'Burglary, perhaps.' There was amused laughter, and the woman who'd spoken before toasted César with her champagne-glass.

'The only things César steals are women's hearts,' she observed. 'But I didn't know you could be jailed for that.'

'Compared to beheading,' César said, 'I suppose jail's a soft option.' His eyes were holding Lola's, his gaze startlingly direct. She dropped her eyes, disturbed by the man's aura.

'I don't believe in reincarnation, anyway,' she said. 'It's just another way for people to blame their own weaknesses and failures on something else.'

'You mean you've never had memories of other times and places?' César asked, still watching her. 'You don't ever find yourself knowing what it was like to live in, say, Roman Britain, or Ancient Greece?'

'I'm too busy surviving in the twentieth century,' she replied, fiddling with her glass. She was itching to be away from him, out of the dangerous nuances of this conversation. Providentially, Mamie signalled to her across the deck, and with a feeling of relief, she excused herself, and made her way over. She could feel a pair of thoughtful golden eyes on her back, and it wasn't a very comfortable feeling.

The day passed peacefully. It wasn't until the sun was low on the horizon, and the sky flooded with red gold, that Lola found herself facing their host again. She'd been leaning over the rail in the stern, staring thoughtfully into the water and thinking about her uncertain future, when she felt a cool touch on her arm.

'A penny for your thoughts?'

She turned with a sinking heart, and found him holding out a martini.

'My thoughts aren't worth your penny,' she said uncommunicatively. She took the drink, thinking uncomfortably how far away the rest of the guests were. He toasted her silently, and watched her with thoughtful eyes over the rim of his glass as he drank.

'You are a very quiet Lola,' he said mildly. 'Someone as lovely as you should be vivacious and self-assertive.'

'It's my job to be quiet,' she shrugged, feeling awkward as the casual compliment sank in. 'Mrs Prenderghast wouldn't keep me long if I habitually made a fuss—even if that was what I wanted, which it definitely isn't.'

'Ah. You're a professional mouse.'

'Not in the slightest,' she snapped angrily, stung by the unexpected taunt. 'I'm a travelling companion—which is quite a different thing!'

'So there is some blood in your veins,' he grinned. 'Then tell me—what makes a highly educated and beautiful woman like Lola Golightly take such a humble job with someone like Mamie Prenderghast?'

'Force of circumstances,' she replied, tasting her drink. It was heady, like the situation. She drew a deep breath. 'And what makes a wealthy, respected man like César Levertov take up grand larceny in his spare time?'

'Grand larceny,' he repeated in his deliciously husky voice, and raised one eyebrow in mock-puzzlement. 'The phrase is an American one, I believe—and foreign to me. My English isn't very good. I'm afraid.'

'It's faultless, and you know it,' she retorted. 'Despite your Russian-French background!'

'Someone's been telling you about my gypsy origins?' he asked.

'Indeed,' she nodded, wishing she was better at this verbal fencing. 'I'm learning quite a bit about the skeletons in your closet.'

'I didn't know there were any,' he said, making it a question.

'How about kleptomania?' she suggested pointedly.

'My Greek isn't very good either,' he said, his eyes bright with unseen laughter.

'If you know that kleptomania's a Greek word, then you know what it means,' she replied. That amused armour of his was almost impossible to dent!

'Skeletons bore me, anyway. I'm more interested in the living.' His eyes caressed her breasts impudently. 'But whence this preoccupation with my background?'

'I'm not remotely interested in your background,' she said tartly, feeling that he was making her look as gauche as a schoolgirl. 'We were discussing grand larceny.'

'We were discussing the circumstances that led you to Mrs Prenderghast's service,' he corrected calmly. 'But we can get to that later. Tell me about grand larceny instead.'

'It means stealing very valuable things,' Lola told him, 'as you perfectly well know!' She was sounding a lot more aggressive than she meant to, and knew that he was enjoying seeing her put on edge like this. His teeth were white and beautifully even, and his smile was genuinely amused.

'My dear Lola! What could poor Mamie have that I would wish to steal?'

'You've been hanging round "poor Mamie's" neck all afternoon,' Lola said acidly. 'Maybe you were studying her diamonds for future reference, who knows?'

'That's jealousy. You're not supposed to be jealous of me,' he said softly. 'We hardly know each other yet.'

'I'm *not* jealous of you!' she snapped in outrage.

'No?' He was infuriatingly calm, his maleness disturbingly close to her. 'Yet I felt an instantaneous attraction towards you, the minute our eyes met. A kind of electric current. Can you deny that you felt it too?'

'I don't kn-know what you're talking about,' she returned, flushing hotly. Her schoolgirl stammer, usually well-buried, was suddenly lurking on her tongue again to trip her words. 'You were only a slave when I was Cleopatra—not Antony!'

'My name is César,' he said gravely. 'And Caesar, if I remember correctly, got Cleopatra in the end. Besides, I wasn't talking about this afternoon.'

'Then you admit you were in Mrs Prenderghast's suite last night?' Lola demanded, wide-eyed at the admission.

'You had a nightmare,' he smiled mockingly. 'Mrs Prenderghast has been amusing us all with the story. As a matter of fact, I did warn her that there might well be a kernel of truth in what you'd said. I said that you didn't look like a dreamer to me.'

'Very am-amusing!'

'What a delicious stammer,' he purred, eyes smoky on her mouth. 'But according to your story, this mystery burglar was masked. How can you possibly connect him with me?'

'Because your eyes are unforgettable,' she snapped.

'There,' he said approvingly, 'I knew you'd felt it too.' He clinked his glass against hers. 'I feel sure that this is the beginning of a meaningful and beautiful friendship.' He didn't have to say a thing to let her know he was laughing at her with rich, wicked amusement.

'I'm going to tell the p-police,' Lola threatened, really angry at the way he was playing with her.

'The p-police would never believe you,' he teased. 'Besides which, *Monsieur le Préfect* happens to have a very high opinion of me. You are not in a strong position, Lola. As a chess-player, I would advise you to make as few moves as possible—until you know which way the game is going.' The sunset was an incendiary aura around them, and he tilted her chin up to study her angry face by its light. 'Your eyes are the colour of rainclouds over the Camargue,' he smiled. 'Angry. You are lovely. And also very troublesome.'

'T-troublesome?' she queried, her self-confidence ebbing away rapidly.

'Ah, that stutter,' he smiled. 'It makes your mouth look so ravishingly innocent. Such a lovely mouth—but by opening it at the wrong moment last night, my dear Lola, you've given me more of a headache than you can possibly guess. I think you owe me some kind of compensation for my trouble—don't you?'

He took the glass from her shaky fingers and tossed it into the sea, then drew her round to face him.

'Don't you dare!' she threatened in alarm.

'Don't what?' he asked silkily.

'Whatever you're going to do,' she said, glancing nervously at the other guests across the deck. 'S-someone may be watching——'

'Everyone's much too busy with the sunset,' he pointed out. He was warm against her, a hint of the iron-hard body beneath reaching her through the fine clothes as his arms slid round her shoulders. And though his formidable strength was restrained, she could no more have resisted it than she could have fought off an avalanche.

The kiss was possessive, his mouth warm and alien against her own. With sudden shock she felt his tongue probe the sweetness of her inner lip, a sexual startlingly erotic invasion. She couldn't stop her body from tensing rigidly against his, her fingernails digging into his shoulders. Dizzily she was aware of his hands pulling her shamelessly close against his powerful body. The texture of his kiss, warm and moist and thrusting, was a physical experience more frighteningly delicious than anything she'd known before.

She jerked away from him furiously, her face scarlet.

'How dare you?' she asked shakily. And then, with theatrical suddenness, the last blinding rim of the sun slipped below the sea, and hazy twilight flooded the sky.

'The sun goes suddenly here in the south,' he said calmly. His expression was one of quietly contained amusement; only the dark fullness of his pupils suggested that he had in any way shared her arousal of a second ago. 'What are you going to do now? Slap my face?'

Lola turned away, feeling too shaky to look into his eyes any longer. She'd been almost shockingly moved a second ago, and anger was now surging into its place. Dimly, she was aware of the other guests turning away from the sunset and glancing towards them. 'Your timing is very good,' she said in a taut voice, her soul still turbulent after what he'd done to her emotions. Bitterness crossed her bruised mouth. 'Was that my punishment for upsetting your plans?'

'Exactly,' he smiled, his eyes reflecting the glory of the departed sun. 'You can't say it was so very unpleasant?'

'It was a damned liberty,' she said evenly. Reaction was making her feel very weak. She glanced across the deck. No one would have been able to see a thing—and if someone were to look their way now, they would see only their glamorous host being his usual gallant self in spending a few minutes talking to the little English nobody called Lola. 'Do you honestly think I won't inform on you now that you've kissed me?'

'Not at all,' he grinned. 'You are free to say whatever you wish to whomsoever you wish.' His eyes dropped to her lips. 'If you really want to make a complete fool of yourself. As a matter of fact, kissing you was something I've been planning to do since the first time I set eyes on you.'

'Damn you!' she snapped. 'I'm not some doll for you to toy with!'

'I hope not,' he grinned. 'I prefer my Cleopatras haughty.' Someone was calling his name from the other end of the deck, and he waved briefly. 'But I'm afraid I must get back to my boring guests.'

He bent over her hand, and the touch of his lips on her skin was almost painful. 'I look forward to our next meeting. Perhaps we'll have more leisure to discuss all this then.'

She snatched her hand away. 'I don't want to discuss *anything* with you, anywhere or anytime!'

But he was already walking away. She watched him, her heart still thudding, and touched her tender lips wonderingly. Infuriating man! What on earth had made him kiss her like that? If his intention had been to get his own back on her for last night, by making her feel a complete idiot yet again—he had certainly succeeded!

Lola leaned back against the rail, trying to recover her balance, and watched him moving among the guests with sure, balanced grace. Easily the most self-confident, forceful man she'd ever met. And one of the most physically impressive, she had to admit. Leaving aside her instinctive antagonism to him, could he *possibly*, after all, have had some genuine motive for being in their apartment in the dead of night? It was so unlikely. If she ever saw him again, though, she vowed, she was going to get some answers!

CHAPTER THREE

THE Bulgarian monster emerged from his door as Lola and Mrs Prenderghast walked towards the lift the next morning. His black eyes darted suspiciously between them, but he made no reply to Lola's cheerful 'Good morning.'

In the lift, Lola studied the bulky, broad-nosed face covertly. Despite his obviously expensive suit, he had none of the grace or style that usually goes with wealth. He smelled strongly of old sweat and rosewater, and the fine cloth fitted his bulky body badly. Mrs Prenderghast's expression clearly showed her outrage at having to share the lift with her old enemy.

'Prenderghast often wore cologne,' she told Lola frigidly round the Bulgarian's rocky shoulder. 'He was in many ways a most effeminate man. I consider the use of perfume a sign of moral weakness in men.'

Fortunately, this sally seemed to go right over the Bulgarian's boulder-shaped head, and they reached the foyer without further incident. As the lift doors opened, the Bulgarian clamped a black felt hat squarely on his head, and strode with his rolling gait to the glass doors. Lola wondered how he was going to spend the day. It was incongruous to imagine that dark, slightly sinister figure innocently sightseeing along the Côte d'Azur, or lying on a beach, complete with black hat.

'I can forgive that odious man for his rudeness,'

Mrs Prenderghast said loudly, 'but I shall never forgive him for stealing our suite.'

Lola's grey-green eyes widened as she watched the Bulgarian leave. A thought had suddenly struck her hard.

'Come along, sweetie,' Mrs Prenderghast said, slipping her arm through Lola's. She'd obviously forgiven Lola for the invisible-burglar incident of the other night.

Lola nodded, coming along. But she was thinking very deeply indeed. The Bulgarian was in *their* suite. . .

Making up her mind, she disengaged her arm from Mamie's. 'I'm just going to have a word with the receptionist—I want to see if the Jenkins sisters have picked up that copy of *Passion's Slave* you signed for them.'

'Well don't be long. We mustn't be late for the taxi, must we? Punctuality is the politeness of princes.'

Lola hurried to the desk, her face intent. There were one or two things she wanted to ask the receptionist. . .

'What did you think of César Levertov?' Mrs Prenderghast asked when Lola returned with the news that the Misses Jenkins had indeed picked up their book. 'Wasn't he the most *charming* man? So cultured, so elegant, so *manly*! People like that, Lola, are very valuable examples to the rest of us.'

'Very valuable,' Lola agreed stiffly. The only things César Levertov could give lessons in were sheer insolence and professional burglary!

'They give us something to look up to. Something to *imitate*.' She gave a breathy sigh, and squeezed Lola's arm intimately. 'I find qualities in César that are sadly lacking in today's men. In fact,' she confided, 'I'm thinking of basing my next hero on him!'

'That sounds a fine idea.' She tried to keep the irony out of her reply. 'He's certainly glamorous enough. I wouldn't trust him an inch, but he's definitely glamorous.'

'Untrustworthy? You think so?' Mamie's painted eyebrows peaked.

'A girlfriend of mine at college warned me never to trust a handsome man,' Lola said, covering her very real antagonism towards the man with a tight smile.

'Untrustworthy or not, you seemed very deep in conversation with him yesterday,' Mrs Prenderghast trilled. 'He's such a very kind and generous person, isn't he? She paused. 'What—what exactly were you talking about?'

'Oh——' Lola looked guilty across at her employer, remembering the feel of César's magnificent body against hers, the leaping of her pulses when he kissed her. 'Nothing, Mrs Prenderghast—just this and that——'

'Come, come.' Roguishly, Mrs Prenderghast pulled Lola to a halt. She was wearing coral-pink again today, and the hairdresser had pulled her hair up into a tinted bouffant hairstyle which, with the dangling jade earrings she was wearing, made her even more noticeable than usual. '*I* know more than "this and that" went on between you.'

'Well——' Inwardly, Lola cursed her pink cheeks.

Mrs Prenderghast shook her finger waggishly at Lola.

'You can't fool Mamie! You and César weren't

just passing the time of day, were you?'

A memory of those wickedly beautiful eyes jolted her senses. 'I—er——'

'He was asking you about me, wasn't he? Wanting to know whether I was still married?' Mrs Prenderghast nodded happily, and set off again, pulling Lola with her. 'I knew he was. I could see at once that he'd been struck by me. Discreet of you to try and hide it from me—but I'm too old a fox to be fooled.' Speechless, Lola could only shake her head in agreement. 'Of course,' Mrs Prenderghast said complacently, 'I'm twenty years too old for him, more's the pity. But it *is* nice to know that one can still make a man's heart beat a *little* faster.' She preened her vast bosom. 'He's such a virile, *impulsive* boy. I shall have to beware of leading him on too much.' She smiled artfully at Lola. 'These strong, passionate men can be so easily hurt, you know.'

Lola gaped, then shut her mouth. Oddly, she found Mrs Prenderghast's vanity not so much amusing as touching, and she gave the plump arm under hers an affectionate squeeze.

'You could turn any man's head,' she said gently.

'Mine has always been a very selective charm,' Mrs Prenderghast said smugly. 'Delicate, rather than dazzling. It takes a man of great taste to appreciate it. But *you* now—you really are a beauty. With those green eyes, and golden hair—a modern Ellen Terry, one might almost say. And you dress so beautifully.' She eyed Lola. 'You didn't really think César was untrustworthy, did you?'

For a moment Lola toyed with the idea of

telling Mrs Prenderghast of her certainty that
César and the midnight burglar were one and the
same man, but rejected the idea decisively. Mamie
would certainly think her insane if she suggested
any such thing!

'I suppose he was very nice,' she said, all but
shrugging.

'You suppose so?' Mrs Prenderghast dabbed at
her lipstick. 'How extraordinary you are sometimes! Why, I thought he was simply divine! So
masculine, so warm——'

'He was very charming,' Lola agreed woodenly,
cutting through the gush. For some reason it
grated on her nerves to hear Mrs Prenderghast
singing César Levertov's praises. The man was a
total fraud!

'What a sphinx you are! Still, if you hadn't been
such a *solemn* creature, I'd never have considered
you as a companion, you know.'

'Am I so solemn?' Lola smiled, relieved to be off
the subject of César.

'Oh, *quite* sphinx-like,' she was assured. 'At first
I was sure you were going to be much too pretty
for peace! But it's very refreshing to find a young
person who doesn't flirt and chatter with every
man in sight the whole time. Some of my
companions have been shockers for that, you
know. Now—where's our taxi?'

Lola went out to find it, wondering whether the
compliment wasn't a rather double-edged one.
What on earth would Tom say if he knew his
once-boisterous sister was being praised for her
sphinx-likeness? And César had called her a
professional mouse yesterday. What's happened to
me? she wondered a little mournfully. She'd been
such a happy person, so untidy and noisy and full

of fun. Had two months of Mamie Prenderghast worn her down this far? Or was she just getting old?

Mrs Prenderghast had asked Lola to arrange to have a taxi drive her on a sightseeing trip round Nice and its environs. It was technically Lola's morning off, but Mrs Prenderghast had conveniently forgotten that. Lola herself would have much preferred walking in the sunshine and the fresh air, but naturally hadn't said so.

Naturally.

There's so much of Mamie, she thought suddenly, that there doesn't seem to be any time at all for *me*.

When she'd accepted this job, she'd had a mental image of seeing all the magnificent Renaissance palaces and gardens that she had spent so long studying and reading about. It had come as rather a disappointment to find that Mrs Prenderghast had only two passions—meeting people in the publishing industry, and being driven round and round in the back of taxis.

The afternoon, at least, had been set aside for a visit to the Baroness Var and another party of editorial and publishing people. That might be a slightly more interesting event. Would César be at the Baroness's? She remembered his promise that they would meet again, and felt her heart sinking at the thought of seeing him again. If he was there, at least she could confront him with what she'd found out at reception that morning. She spotted the grey Peugeot that was waiting for them.

The driver embarked on a long and obviously well-rehearsed speech about the beauties of Nice as soon as they'd settled themselves inside, and he kept up his commentary almost non-stop, which allowed Lola to sit back and let the tide of his words wash over her as the car ambled along the sunwashed boulevards.

She thought of the letter she'd written to her father last night, after they'd got back from the yacht. *'Was introduced to a real live Count,'* she'd written, *'though apparently a modern one. Very glamorous and handsome. The sunset was marvellous. . .'* She hadn't mentioned the fact that the real live Count was also her golden-eyed burglar of the night before. Or the fact that he'd kissed her as she'd never been kissed before. She thought of the Bulgarian's sinister black hat again, and shook her head. César Levertov was a man of mystery, and that was undeniable!

Mrs Prenderghast's commanding voice broke into her reverie, and Lola filed her thoughts away for the time being, and composed herself to being the dutiful companion again.

The Baroness Var's mansion was on the coast, nearer Marseilles than Nice.

A colonnade of towering palms extended in two broad curves from the sweeping white lines of the house, and an assortment of guests' cars had been parked under their criss-cross shade. The house itself was old, and its contents were aristocratic, rather battered, and smelled rather musty. There were four or five big dogs in the same condition, and as soon as Lola walked into the house, a wave of nostalgia swept over her.

The place was a French, much grander version of a house she'd spent some of the happiest days of her childhood in—her Aunt Leila's farmhouse, in Devon. There was exactly the same sleepy impression of a bygone summer, the same slow fly or two, the same dogs, the same fine furniture gone to seed, the same cabinets full of antique china—and the Baroness herself, a smiling white-haired lady with shortsighted blue eyes, even hobbled on two sticks the way Aunt Leila had done.

Lola had been expecting some slim, fashionable creature loaded with gold and diamonds. It was an unexpected delight to find Aunt Leila resurrected in the form of a slightly shabby old patrician with manners as exquisite and old-fashioned as the cool china in the cabinets.

And, curiously, it was as thought she somehow shared Lola's odd sense of recognition.

'What *beautiful* hair,' she smiled at Lola, before the hovering Mme Roche could make any introductions, and reached out to caress the swathe of dark gold. 'My daughter has hair like that. And such a sweet face——'

'Miss Golightly,' Mrs Prenderghast cut in, her voice bristling at this *lèse-majesté*, 'is my *companion*, Baroness.'

'Ah, Mrs Prenderghast,' beamed the Baroness, turning to the author, 'it's such a pleasure to meet you. I've enjoyed every one of your books, Madame! And now that you are being translated into French, of course, I rejoice that so many of my countrywomen will experience that same pleasure.'

Lola had to suppress a smile as the answering beam spread across her employer's brightly painted face. Nothing could have been better calculated to put Mamie in a good mood. She glanced covertly round the huge drawing-room. No sign of César among the several guests. Relief lightened her heart. She'd been rather dreading meeting him here!

'Now come,' the Baroness was saying, 'and rest yourselves in the cool.' Again, she reached out to touch Lola's hair. 'And bring your charming companion,' she smiled as they accompanied her hobbling figure. 'Such a very pretty face. Do all the young men chase after you, child?'

'I'm afraid not, Baroness,' Lola replied.

'No beaux waiting for you in rainy England?'

'None,' Lola smiled. 'As soon as we get back to England I shall have to start trying to find a job—maybe in teaching, or archaeology.'

'A job?' Old-fashioned disapproval crossed the lined, kindly face. 'You must get married,' the Baroness said firmly, 'and give those green eyes and that golden hair to your children. Marriage is a woman's glory—as I'm sure Mrs Prenderghast tells you.'

'Lola's not interested in that sort of thing,' Mrs Prenderghast volunteered with a titter. 'I was saying only this morning what a little sphinx she is. Doesn't seem to care for men at all.'

'That's not true,' the Baroness decided, nodding at Lola, whose cheeks were by now beginning to go pink. 'Is it? Not with looks like that. Lola has a woman's heart. I shall have to find you a husband, my dear!'

She led them to the other guests and the usual round of small-talk, and the party settled down to an aperitif before lunch.

The lunch passed pleasantly, served by two butlers of the same vintage as the Baroness, and Mrs Prenderghast was again the centre of attention. True to form, Lola concentrated on her sphinx-like act on the fringes, though she was conscious of the many warm smiles the Baroness threw her way from time to time. There seemed almost to be a secret between them, a common understanding.

It was much later, at around three in the afternoon, when everyone had settled in the shade of an arbour in the Countess's gloriously untidy rose-garden, that Lola heard a chorus of welcomes, and looked up suddenly to see César Levertov's tall figure coming down the stone steps. Her heart jumped violently inside her at the sight of him, but he didn't seem to even notice her as he greeted the hostess, apparently an old friend, and Mrs Prenderghast.

'Excuse my formal clothes, Elaine,' she heard him saying, 'I've come straight from work. Sorry I couldn't make it earlier.'

Work? What work, she wondered? He was wearing a beautiful charcoal-grey suit and a red silk tie, and looked, Lola thought, like the director of some big company. He'd come, she guessed, in a Rolls or a Bentley.

He had been in sheer black the first time she'd seen him, frightening and electrifying. The second time, he'd been in the immaculate cream-and-white uniform of a Riviera playboy. Now, in the conservatively cut suit, complete with hand-made shoes and silk shirt, yet a third side of his personality was highlighted—the authoritative, strong-willed man of affairs, used to making decisions and giving orders. She knew the look— the senior directors in her father's company had it, an aura of capability, of experience.

Which was the real César Levertov? Maybe there wasn't an answer to that question. God, he was handsome! Flirting outrageously with Mrs Prenderghast, Lola watched the way his big, lean body moved, the tilt of his head. The dark hair would grow thick and long if he'd let it, but it was clipped slightly shorter than was fashionable, giving him an almost military air of neat ruthlessness.

Whether playboy or thief or hard-working director, she couldn't keep her eyes off him. Only once did the amber eyes, with their fringe of dark lashes, glance her way, and probe her very soul. He seemed to have something to say to everyone, much to Lola's frustration—and it was a long while before he drifted over to where she was sitting in the fragrant shade of a briar-rose.

'You're even lovelier than yesterday,' he smiled quietly. 'I like you better with your hair let down. You look too spinsterish with it up.'

'I am a spinster,' she reminded him coolly. He sat beside her, his presence seeming to quicken her whole being.

'Have you had any more nightmares?' he asked with a gleam of amusement in his eyes.

'None,' she replied, not rising to the bait. 'But I've been putting two and two together—and making some enquiries.'

'Indeed!'

'Indeed.'

'And what have you concluded?' he smiled, leaning back on one elbow.

Lola drew a breath to steady herself. 'You weren't after Mrs Prenderghast's diamonds at all, were you?' she asked calmly.

He raised his eyebrows. 'Was I not?'

'No. It came to me this morning, in the lift. I can't think why I didn't realise it before. There was a mix-up with the rooms at the Grande, you see. When we arrived, they'd already given suite 223 to someone else. A Bulgarian man, who'd arrived the day before. His name is Akhtopol.' She glanced at him. He hadn't reacted to the name—she'd found it out at the reception that morning—but the laughter in the bronzed face seemed stilled by what she'd said. 'He's some kind of airline executive. He's here to attend an aviation technology congress. That's what the manager says, anyway. And Mme Roche said you had something to do with airplanes. I don't understand all that. But you didn't know about the mix-up,' she went on. 'You thought you were burgling Mr Akhtopol's room, didn't you?'

He didn't deny it, just watched her with intent, disturbing eyes.

'Aren't you going to tell me I must be crazy?' she challenged. 'This is the second time I've accused you of breaking and entering, after all.'

'No,' he said, his expression thoughtful. 'You've been very clever to work it out.'

So—she was finally approaching the truth! 'You must have been rather surprised to find me there,' Lola went on, thinking with amusement of what he must have felt on seeing her in the room. 'Who did you think I was?'

'Mr Akhtopol's bedmate,' he answered calmly, and then grinned at her discomfiture. 'Such things go on in big hotels. And you looked very fetching in that négligé.' He studied her simple print dress critically. 'It's the only garment I've ever seen you in that showed any flair, as a matter of fact.'

'I don't dress for men to ogle me,' she replied tartly, her cheeks reddened by the sexy expression on that stunningly attractive mouth. It reminded her acutely of that shocking kiss!

'How virtuous. And what else have you worked out, little sleuth?'

'Not much,' she admitted cautiously. She was pleased that her theory had proved correct. 'I'd love to know what you've got against poor Mr Akhtopol that you should risk your life burgling his suite?'

César smiled. '"Poor Mr Akhtopol" isn't an airline executive, Lola. He's one of the East European executives of a very big aero-engineering consortium. And he has something that I want very badly.'

'Then you *are* a burglar!'

'How can I deny the charge?' His grin was disarming. 'In my own defence, though, I must tell you that what Mr Akhtopol has was originally stolen from me.'

'Something valuable?' she probed, not at all sure whether he wasn't spinning her a complicated line.

'Potentially.' He snapped a rose off the overhanging shrub, and sniffed it absently. 'I run a company called Aero-Mediterranean—Aeromed for short. We build executive jets, small transport aircraft, and a number of aerospace components.' He shrugged. 'As you can imagine, the plans for some of these things are worth a lot of money to the right people.'

'Are you saying that Mr Akhtopol has stolen one of your designs?' she asked sceptically.

'He bought a design,' César corrected, 'that was taken from my factory illegally.' Despite the heat and his formal suit, he looked enviably cool and crisp. He dropped the rose into Lola's lap, and smiled with amber-flecked eyes. 'You look uncertain, lovely Lola.'

'I don't know whether to believe you or not,' she said, biting her lower lip. Her instinct was to distrust every syllable he uttered!

'Come for a stroll with me among Elaine's beautiful roses,' he invited, 'and I'll convince you.'

'I'm not sure I should even be listening to you,' she said reluctantly. Nevertheless, she rose when he did, and followed him between the vivid beds of butterfly haunted roses. He slid his arm casually through hers, and she felt the sinewy strength of his body against her own slenderness. It was hard not to flinch away, but she didn't want to risk being teased any more.

'In an industry like aerospace, my dear Lola, the current technology expands every day.' He glanced at her. 'Have you heard of the Lincoln 2000?'

She searched her mind. 'It's some kind of aeroplane, isn't it?'

'Exactly. A ten-seater executive jet. The Lincoln has been our main production plane at Aeromed for the past four years. It's been a very good seller indeed—but a good design doesn't last for ever, and in the meantime, I've been working on the successor to the Lincoln, a plane we've tentatively called the Churchill.'

It was evidence of his megalomania, she thought with amusement, to name his creations after the statesmen who'd shaped world history!

He sensed her amusement, and smiled without rancour. 'It sounds very grand to call them after famous men. We also make a high-performance six-seater called the Richelieu. At any rate, by the time we had the first Churchill prototype, we'd become very excited. I spent many hundreds of hours flying the plane myself, ironing out the kinks, adjusting, refining, correcting. And in the end we knew we had something that was going to outperform and undersell almost every form of executive transport in the air. More than that, in fact. The design has applications for all kinds of things, not just executive transport. It can be used on almost any medium-scale function, from military observation planes to small commercial cargo freighters. A winner.' A rueful expression crossed his mouth. 'Which was when all our troubles started.'

'Why?' Lola demanded, caught up in the tale, 'surely it was fantastic news for you?'

'Yes,' he nodded, 'but not such good news for the other people in the aerospace industry, especially the giants like Cirrus Aviation. For them, our design breakthrough meant a lot of headaches. A big cut in sales, for one thing. For another, they had to face the prospect of re-gearing all their design programmes to keep pace with the Churchill and all the Churchill-class planes that would soon be taking over the executive market. That also meant having to pay, in all probability, vast sums of money to us for the use of our patents. And finally, it meant having to take a back seat while Aeromed, a relatively small newcomer, forged ahead into the forefront of the aviation industry.'

Lola nodded her understanding, feeling a thrill of excitement as she imagined how César and his team must have felt. 'So how did Mr Akhtopol get his hands on the plans for the Churchill?' she asked.

'Quite simply.' The sea of roses was headily perfumed, and the voices of the other guests were only a drowsy murmur behind them. He led her to an old garden bench, and they sat down next to a snowy bed of Iceberg. They were completely hidden from the rest of the party. She watched his lean, tanned face with fascinated eyes as he went on.

He picked up her hand, and spread her slim fingers out against his own palm, studying the satiny skin. The highly distracting contact made her shiver, but he didn't seem to notice her reaction. 'Cirrus,' he went on thoughtfully, stroking the lines of her hand gently, 'is a cartel of powerful businessmen who have a very big stake in the aviation industry. They stood to lose a lot of sales, time, and prestige because of us. So they came up with what they told us was an offer we couldn't refuse. They wanted to buy the Churchill patents from us, do all the developing and marketing themselves, and cut us in for a stake in the profits. All we had to do was sit back and rake in the millions.'

'Wasn't that an attractive offer?' Lola asked in puzzlement.

César's eyes blazed gold. 'Not to me,' he said coolly. 'Aero Mediterranean is my company. And the Churchill is *my* design. Maybe you think I'm a pampered aristocrat, who's always had things his own way.' Muscles tightened across the hard, ruthless jawline. 'I'm not, Lola. I started with less than nothing. My parents were beautiful, charming people—but their heads were full of romantic rubbish. They were totally impractical.' He shook his head ruefully. 'Time had stood still for them. My grandfather was partly to blame—he led them to believe that the Bolsheviks only had to fall for them to be invited back to rule Russia in wealth and splendour, as though 1917 had never happened. They didn't have a single sensible thought between them. And when they died— young, luckily, before the twentieth century had

had much time to destroy their illusions—they left me only their debts. There was no château, no estates, no financial empire—nothing like that. I was sixteen, and I had to work to pay for my own bed and board before I could even think of starting to work my way through engineering college in Paris. Even when I won a research grant to study in America for four years, it didn't come easy.' His fingers laced through hers, and she felt their steely strength as they bit into her hand. 'I won't bore you with the details. But I built Aeromed out of a garage in a Marseilles dockland. And every new design I came up with, every revolutionary notion—I had to struggle for it, drag it out of my guts and work day and night to bring it to reality. Slowly, I assembled a team who thought as I did, who were prepared to sacrifice themselves and drive themselves the way I did— for the sake of a dream.' He smiled into her eyes. 'A dream of success, financial independence. A dream of getting to the top. Do you think I could really stand back now, just when that dream has finally become true, and hand my plans tamely over to some huge conglomerate—and watch *them* suck everything in, all the hard work and inspiration, all the prestige and acclaim?' He shook his head with a soft laugh. 'I'm too wilful and ambitious a man for that.'

Lola nodded again, watching the strength so evident in that handsome face. 'I begin to see,' she said slowly. 'So what happened?'

'Almost everyone on my board of directors thought exactly the same way,' he said with a slightly bitter shrug. 'Except for two men who were eager to get their hands on a lot of money, fast. They'd been hypnotised by Cirrus's offer, and they put up a long argument. Why should we struggle and work to make the Churchill a success ourselves, they asked, when someone else can do the job for us? We've worked for seven years to build Aeromed. Why not just retire in comfort, and let Cirrus provide us with a free meal-ticket for the rest of our lives? Nor did it make any difference to them when I pointed out that by developing Churchill ourselves we could make infinitely more than the nine or ten million a year Cirrus were offering.'

'I think I sympathise with them,' Lola said with a slight smile. 'Ten million sounds an awful lot to me.'

'Okay,' he admitted wryly, leaning back, 'there was much more to it than money. Accepting Cirrus's offer was tantamount to voting Aeromed out of existence—and all of us out of jobs! With me, it was a question of pride more than anything else. To someone who has worked for everything he has in this life, taking a back seat can never be an attractive proposition—no matter how luxurious that back seat may be. I love aeroplanes, you see. Until I have children of my own, my designs are my children. And I want to build that plane to my own specifications, not to see it bastardised and homogenised in some mass-production line.'

'So you told them to shove it?' Lola asked inelegantly, stirred by the fierce independence of the man.

'I advised my board to reject the offer,' he corrected her amusedly. 'Yes. And but for the two men in question, they all agreed. One of the two is a man of honour, and accepted the majority decision. The other——' The bronzed face tightened. 'The other, Herbert Poincarré, decided to make his own deal—in private—with Cirrus. A private fortune in exchange for the purloined Churchill designs. He stole what he could, without anyone knowing, and——'

'And sold it to Mr Akhtopol?' Lola finished eagerly.

'I am sure he did,' César nodded. 'The Côte d'Azur Airshow is one of the biggest aviation technology conferences in the world. I couldn't attend this year, because I was too busy with the Churchill—so I asked Poincarré to delegate for me. Ironic. It gave him the perfect cover to meet Akhtopol—who is a big-shot on the Cirrus executive committee—and come to some kind of deal.'

'Why didn't you go to the police?' Lola demanded. 'You said that the *Préfect* was a friend of yours.'

'For one thing,' he replied, his eyes laughing at her frustrated expression, 'I have very little proof that my friend Poincarré actually has sold the design. All the designs are stored on computers, and all I can prove is that Poincarré made a secret copy of one of the master-tapes. As a member of the Aeromed board, he naturally has free access to all design and planning material—only selling such material is a crime, and it may be very hard to prove that he did so. For another, the law is cumbersome and slow. It has to go through the proper channels and steer round all the obstacles. Computerisation means that by the time the law got around to even questioning Mr Akhtopol, he could have transmitted the information telephonically to his colleagues in Brussels or Dortmund or Sofia.' He took a slim panatella from his pocket, and unwrapped it slowly. 'I should be very surprised if he has not already done so.'

'Oh, no,' Lola said miserably.

'Oh, yes. Burglarising Mr Akhtopol's suite—or what I thought was Mr Akhtopol's suite—was a spontaneous gamble. It occurred to me that I might just find the computer tape in his suite.'

'And what if he happened to hear you and wake up?' she asked nervously.

'I was an angry man,' he said mildly. 'And I might even have welcomed a meeting with Mr Akhtopol to—express my feelings.' He touched her lips softly. 'As I say, a gamble. What little chance I had was effectively ruined when you opened that delicious mouth and screamed.' He chuckled at her horror. 'I'm used to taking chances, Lola, and seeing them fail now and then. Don't feel too bad. It was a pleasant night for climbing, anyhow. The sea is good, but I was born in Briançon, and I miss the Alps here in Nice.'

'You must be a very experienced climber,' Lola said, still feeling very guilty.

'I was on the French Olympic team two years ago.' He exhaled a fragrant cloud of cigar-smoke. 'The burglary itself was boringly simple. My foreman took an apartment four floors above yours the day before, under a false name. I went up with my climbing gear, dressed as an electrician. When I judged the time was right, I simply abseiled down, and found an unlatched window. After our—er—encounter, I hauled myself back up again.'

She shuddered at the thought of the moonlit chasm of the hotel's sheer side. 'So that's how you appeared and disappeared so amazingly. They all thought I was seeing things!'

'Serves you right,' he retorted drily. 'But for you, my problems might all be over by now.'

She hesitated, flushing. Was he telling the truth or not? Instinctively, she knew he was, and she laid her hand lightly on his arm.

'I wasn't to know that you weren't after Mrs Prenderghast's manuscript,' she reminded him apologetically.

'You've made it up to me to some extent,' he said wickedly, and her flush deepened, thinking of yesterday's kiss.

'What are you going to do now?' she asked to cover her confusion.

'Well,' he said through a cloud of aromatic smoke, 'there's not much I *can* do now. Mr Akhtopol was thoroughly alarmed, and probably put two and two together, just as you did. So he now knows—or at least strongly suspects—that I am aware of Poincarré's treachery. He will, if he has the sense I credit him with, try and transfer the information to his executive as soon as he can.'

'What about copyright?' Lola demanded. 'Can't you sue them if they produce a design identical to yours?'

'Maybe. It's certainly my best hope now. They won't make an identical plane, though. They'll simply claim to have discovered the new technology at the same time I did.' He shrugged. 'I rather doubt whether I can reach them effectively through the law—and it's a formidably costly business, as you probably know.'

'I don't know how to tell you how awful I feel,' she said again.

'No matter now.' He caressed the dark gold tresses of her hair, his eyes warm. 'The leak is serious, but not actually disastrous. Poincarré stole the designs for the turbocharging system, and the related cooling systems, which are by no means the whole Churchill story. Cirrus will be able to make up a lot of leeway—but we should still have the master-hand, if we are lucky. And I've severely curtailed computer access,' he smiled grimly. 'No one gets to study those tapes whom I do not trust utterly.'

'What about Poincarré?' Lola asked.

'He flew to America last night, leaving his wife and two children. Akhtopol must have said something to him. I no longer care about Poincarré, in any case. He is not worth my anger. No doubt I shall meet him again some day.' His expression was calm, but Lola felt a chill touch her spine. César Levertov wouldn't be an easy man to cross, and she felt a touch of pity for the hapless Poincarré, who was no doubt now finding the leisure to repent his decision.

'So it's all over?' Lola asked in a small voice.

'For the time being. We're rushing ahead with the production of the first Churchills. They're coming out in two forms, the 7600 and 9000, and we have plenty of orders for both. We shall simply have to wait and see how much Cirrus can work out of the whole design from the plans they have. It'll take them a very long time to be able to build a successful rip-off version of their own, though—and we'll probably have some legal come-back.' With an effort of will, he seemed to shrug the burden of worry from his broad shoulders, and crushed the cigar out under his foot. 'It's not a disaster. Let's drop all that for the time being. I've worried about it long enough, and I'll be worrying about it again—but for now the whole thing sickens me.'

'I'm sorry,' she said a third time, helplessly wishing she could give him some kind of comfort.

'Don't be. There's more to life than the occasional mistake or betrayal.' He ran his hand through his crisp, dark hair, and smiled gently, lines forming at the corners of his eyes. 'I should be grateful to Poincarré for being the means of bringing you and me together.'

'Even after all the trouble I've caused you?' she asked wryly.

He laughed softly. 'The mistake was mine. Besides, you were very brave in screaming like that. I might have had a gun or a knife. I'm the one who owes the apology, Lola. I had no right to start involving you in my private quarrels. Look, I'd love to be able to show the Churchill off to you. And I want to get to know you a great deal better than this. Will you come out to the factory with me sometime soon, and see the Churchill in production? Say the day after tomorrow?'

'I don't think I can,' she said uneasily. Nothing would have been more exciting! But her employer would raise hell. 'Mrs Prenderghast would blow a gasket if I went off anywhere on my own—and besides, she's convinced she's the object of your desires. That's because you've been flattering her so outrageously,' she accused with a slight scowl.

'I wanted to be sure she'd want to see me again,' he grinned, showing beautiful white teeth. 'So that I could be sure of seeing *you* again.'

'You're wicked!' she accused, shocked at his duplicity. Had he really meant that, or was it pure flirtation?

'Nonsense. Mamie enjoys the game as much as I do. She knows it isn't serious, and she must guess that it's you I'm really interested in. Besides—it'll enliven what must be a very dull trip for her. Very well,' he said, gurgling with laughter at her wide eyes, 'I shall invite both you and your literary employer to see my Churchill. Okay?'

'Okay,' she nodded, trying to resist the delight surging inside her. She'd never met anyone as forceful—or as resourceful—as César before. Nor—and that was odd considering what an unorthodox approach he had to life—could she remember anyone as direct and honest. Occasional burglar and con-man he might be, but there was something very direct and singleminded about Monsieur Levertov! 'I l-look forward to that.'

'Why do you stutter every time I'm near you?' he asked. 'Do I make you so nervous?'

'Not at all,' she lied unhappily. 'It's just a schoolgirl h-habit that comes back now and th-then.'

'But you are no longer a schoolgirl,' he said, his eyes drifting to the swell of her breasts against the light cotton. 'Have you got a job lined up when you get back to England?' he asked. She shook her head, thinking with a pang of the gloomy prospect awaiting her when she left this summery paradise. 'Good,' he said briskly. 'I'm coming to England very soon. I want to start marketing the Churchill there. I think the design—and the name, of course—will make it sell well there, especially now that the economy's on the upsurge again. Will you agree to see me then?'

'I—I don't know,' she said. But she felt so outrageously happy inside that she followed that up instantly with, 'Yes!' She couldn't doubt that he really wanted to see her. This wasn't a man who said things lightly—and for all the image he projected of a dangerously irresponsible playboy, he was one of the strongest, most authoritative men she'd ever known.

Suddenly, it was as though her doubts of the morning, her feeling of desolation, had never been. She'd never felt happier than now, never felt so close to anyone, so aware of the potential beauty of life. Her feelings about César Levertov had undergone a radical change over the past half-hour! Impulsively, she slipped her arms round his neck, and kissed him tentatively on the lips. His eyes widened for a second as the warm velvet of her mouth touched his inexpertly, and then he drew her into his arms as naturally, as wonderfully, as though he'd been doing it all his life.

'I'm almost glad you were awake that night,' he said quietly, his mouth against her hair. 'We might not have paid each other nearly as much attention otherwise. . .'

He kissed her softly, his hands drawing her close to him, stroking the slim shape of her body under the light summer dress. Their tongues met, touched, caressed with a heart-stopping passion that made them both draw back, shuddering, to stare into one another's eyes.

Mrs Prenderghast's voice floated to them on the lazy breeze from the arbour.

'Lola! Lola!'

'We have to go,' he said, releasing her unwillingly. 'Let's go and inform your honoured employer that she's been invited to view my masterwork. Who knows? She may even decide to buy one.' Feeling distinctly weak, Lola smiled up at him as he clasped her hand in his, and walked with him towards the arbour.

What shadow could possibly cloud the perfect beauty of this afternoon?

CHAPTER FOUR

In fact, on the morning of their visit to the factory two days later, a thunderstorm broke, and the spell of fine weather gave way to torrential rain which lashed down on the hills and the beaches and the streets of the city of Nice. Not that any amount of rain could have drenched her happiness right now! César picked them up at ten-thirty from the hotel, and Lola felt her spirits soaring at the sight of him. That familiar jolt of electricity was as strong as ever.

It was good to be driving through the countryside towards Antibes, where César's factory was sited. The Aeromed complex was in the countryside some distance from the town. It was impressively large as they breasted the hill overlooking it, consisting of five ultra-modern factory buildings, set against a landscaped parkland six miles from the sea, and a number of aircraft hangars adjoining a long airstrip that stretched towards the horizon through huge fields of what looked like geraniums.

'They're grown for the perfume industry,' César explained as he drove them towards the main workshop. He slid the electric window down, and the rainy air carried a heady breath of bruised geranium leaves into the car. 'Most French perfume is based on geranium essence. Aeromed has a fragrant setting, as you see,' he smiled.

The workshop was an astounding place, its vast floor-space crowded with equipment and overalled

78

workers. The fuselages of three airplanes were
nearing completion in the centre of the floor, and
as César escorted them along the marked
walkways, teams of men were riveting sections of
anodised aluminium on to the sleek cylindrical
bodies. Everything, Lola noticed, was scrupulously
clean. The polished metal surfaces gleamed in the
light from massive louvred windows in the roof,
and the atmosphere of the place was eager,
efficient. The factory manager, an exquisitely
dressed little man with white hair and beard called
Henri Duval, was waiting to meet them in the
office. He gave Lola and Mrs Prenderghast heel-
clicking bows, like a cavalry officer, and gave a
brief report in reply to César's, *'Ça va, Henri?'*
Henri Duval's immaculate pinstripe was a beautifully cut garment, Lola noticed, matched only by
the modern three-piece in charcoal wool that
fitted César's tall frame to perfection. Did all
French businessmen dress like fashion models?
Lola was beginning to feel that her own grey-and-
white suit—bought in Marks and Spencer's last
spring sale, and once her pride and joy—was
scarcely adequate for the occasion.

The relationship between Duval and César was
clearly an excellent one, based on mutual respect.

'Henri has been with us for the past five years,'
he explained, 'for three of which he's been
technically retired.' He put his hand affectionately
on the older man's shoulder. 'But we'd be lost
without Henri, so we pay him a fortune to stay
locked up here in Workshop A.'

In this setting, César's mask of lazy arrogance
had vanished utterly, revealing the real strength of
the man. The vitality in him seemed to hum in
tune with the complicated, sophisticated machinery

all around, and his command of the whole organisation was obviously total. It was incredible to think that there were five other workshops, similar to this one, all working to full capacity—and all the products of one man's brain and determination. Mamie caught Lola's eye and gave a little head-shake of wonderment; Aeromed was obviously a highly geared, highly successful factory, and must certainly be making César Levertov and his team extremely wealthy men.

A cage-lift took them high above the shop floor to a long gantry that overlooked the lines of machinery. A service machine provided paper cups of surprisingly good coffee, and from this rather dizzy height, César explained briefly how the building process was carried out.

'It's like something from the distant future,' Mrs Prenderghast marvelled, peering down at the busy panorama below.

'The technology isn't all that complicated,' César said deprecatingly. 'It's a matter of simple logic.' But the gleam in his eyes told Lola how immensely proud of his organisation he really was. 'These are Richelieus,' he told her, waving his cup at the aircraft below, '—six-seaters with very powerful jet engines. Designed for long distance, high-speed travel. They're on order from America, n'est-ce-pas, Henri?'

'Oui,' the manager nodded, 'these go to the directors of a big oil company.' He gave a Gallic shrug. 'Naturally, such people demand very luxurious specifications.'

Mamie's crocodile-skin notebook was in her hand, a sure sign that she was fascinated, and she scribbled rapidly as Henri described the fittings of the airplanes to her. Lola felt César's fingers close round her arm, and she looked shyly up at him. His eyes probed her face. 'Well?' he asked. 'What are you thinking behind those green eyes?'

'It's staggering,' she said quietly, wanting him to know how deeply impressed she'd been by this sight. 'And somehow quite beautiful. So much work, so much co-ordination—I didn't expect all this.'

'Good,' he said cheerfully. 'And you haven't seen our new baby yet.'

'The Churchill?'

'She's still top-secret,' he said, locking his arm firmly through hers, 'but I don't think Mamie will sell us out to our competitors. If you've finished your coffee, let's go and see her.

The Churchill was in the last hangar, right on the runway, and they had to walk two hundred yards in the fine misty rain, sharing umbrellas. They stood on the shiny-wet tarmac and stared silently at the aircraft that crouched within. It was a magnificent creation by any terms. The vivid image burned itself into Lola's mind—a sleek silver dart with swept-back delta wings, the massive single jet engine poised so aggressively on the fuselage in front of the razor-edged tail.

In the softer lights of the hangar, uncluttered by the massively technical machinery of the factory, it was like something from another planet, a gleaming machine built to defy time itself. Five or six mechanics had been working on the plane as they approached, and now the engines started up, a characteristic jet-whine that climbed steadily to a roar. The backblast was buffeting around the hangar as César led them in, and Lola had to hold on to her whipping hair. She was beginning to see why most of the workers wore caps with earmuffs!

She didn't even try to understand all the specifications and technological details that César's foreman proudly regaled them with, shouting to be heard over the engine's note. Two things were riveted into her imagination—the beautiful, almost terrible power of the craft, like a lightning-bolt waiting to be unleashed, and the expression of pride on César's tanned face as he stared at it, his dark brows curving down. She knew she'd never forget either impression.

The Churchill was deceptively big, its cockpit looming high over their heads as they walked beneath it. 'It's almost like a fighter,' Lola shouted, marvelling at the mirror-smooth surface, the attention to detail that extended even to the finely made aluminium ladder that led up to the interior of the plane.

'That isn't such a fanciful idea,' César said, his mouth close to her ear. 'The Churchill could easily be used in a training role for fighter pilots.' He smiled. 'But as you'll see, it's been designed with comfort, rather than warfare, in mind.' He steered them up the ladder into the interior.

Henri Duval thumped the door shut behind them, cutting off the roar of the engine and muting it to a comfortable level. The utter luxury of the plane's interior, all leather and plush and velvety drapes, left both Lola and Mrs Prenderghast dreamy-eyed, and Lola felt instinctively that César had not exaggerated. The plane was a world-beater, one of the most exciting things she'd ever seen. Millionaires would be queueing to own this ultimate vilirity- and status-symbol!

'You like it?'

He didn't need any answer; their rapt faces said it all. He was grinning as he eased himself into the pilot's seat and reached up for the headset. Lola's eyes widened into excited green pools as she watched him flick the banks of switches with practised fingers, bringing an array of winking dials to life.

'You—you're not going to fly it?' she asked, coming up to examine the technological cavern of the cockpit.

'Of course.' His expression was wicked. 'You didn't think I'd brought you all this way for nothing?'

'César!'

'My ground crew have spent the whole morning getting her ready. Unless you don't feel like flying today?'

Mamie squealed indignantly. 'I wouldn't miss this for worlds! What a *fabulous* idea! I trust we're going to be safe, César?'

'You could trust me with a new-born babe,' he replied gravely, and Mamie nodded satisfaction.

'Good. Where do I sit?'

'*S'il vous plait*, Madame——' Henri guided her to one of the executive-style seats that had been spaciously set out in the passenger area, and stooped to buckle her bulky frame into it.

'This won't be a long flight,' César apologised. 'The Churchill has a busy schedule today. But I'll take you just far enough to give you a general idea of the plane's capabilities.' He nodded his head at the seat beside him. 'I'm giving you a grandstand view, Lola.' His eyes met hers with a glitter of dark amusement. 'To compensate for the fright I gave you the other night. Sit there.' Her heart was beating fast with excitement.

'Shouldn't Henri be here beside you?'

'You can move if anything goes wrong.' His

smile went straight to her heart, the way it was meant to, instantly creating a private world, just for the two of them. He held up the seatbelt for her, and she slipped eagerly into the leather seat. Through the perspex window she could see the Churchill's nose, tapered to a needle point and aimed at the misty horizon ahead. She strapped herself in, and twisted to look behind. Henri and Mamie were beside each other, and by the expression on Mamie's pink face, she was thrilled as a schoolgirl.

César went steadily through the pre-flight checks. Her eyes were on his hands, sure and expert among the hundreds of labelled switches. She'd seen experts before, and knew instinctively that his feeling for the plane was intimate, masterful—and complete. They had very little to fear, she was sure of that. One of the ground crew was signalling with a pair of batons, and the engine climbed a notch under his careful hands. The jet rolled slowly forward as the chocks were taken from under the wheels. Watching the signals with narrowed eyes, he guided the plane out on to the tarmac. A crackle of radio was audible now, and he was talking softly in French into the microphone that curved round in front of his mouth.

Lola was dry-mouthed with excitement. It was completely characteristic of César Levertov, she was beginning to realise, to love springing surprises like this on people—and this was a surprise she could never have anticipated! A few minutes later, the plane was poised on the runway, aimed like a silver spear. There was an interminable pause as César waited for the go-ahead from the air-controller at Nice. Finally, the voice crackled in the headset, and he glanced across at her, his eyes bright.

'Here we go.'

The signaller, informed through his own headset, raised both batons, then walked out of the jet's path. The howl of the engine deepened savagely, thrusting the jet forward. Lola felt her nails dig into her palms with tension. She'd flown in airliners, but this acceleration was unbelievable, forcing her back against the seat like a giant hand as the runway began to hurtle beneath them. It was terrifying, exhilarating, a crescendo of speed that turned the world into an elongated blur, thundering in her ears and vibrating in her spine. The wet tarmac swept by. And then the wheels had left the ground. The vibration was gone; she could hear the wheels clunking into their bays almost immediately as the Churchill climbed steeply, almost vertically, into the rain. The incredible thrust of power lifted them into the mass of white cloud within minutes. She glanced across at the bronzed, aquiline profile. This was *his* creation, this hurtling machine. His fingers were sure on the controls, his nostrils flaring with the joy of flight. He looked at her quickly, then checked his instruments.

'Scared?'

'A l-little,' she confessed with a shaky laugh. The whiteness of her knuckles amplified that understatement eloquently. Cloud plummeted around the windscreen, whipping it with tendrils of water, and then they were deep inside the white barrier. At once, all sense of speed vanished; only the thrust against her back told her they were still climbing fast, surging upwards. She turned to look at Mamie. She was staring intently out of the window, her pursy mouth open with fascination. She'd travelled on the Lord knew how many airline flights, Lola guessed, but this was very definitely a different experience for her. This incident was clearly going to turn up in her next novel in one form or another.

Exploding into the sun was such a startling experience that Lola gasped out loud. The jet burst out of the cloud-layer into a sky that was Wedgwood-blue above them, the blaze of the sun warming the cockpit like a benediction. It was one of the most startlingly beautiful transitions she'd ever known. For a few seconds the white-hot light was intolerable as César seemed to be guiding the jet into the very heart of the sun, and then they were banking in a tight curve, and beginning to level off. Clinging to the armrests, Lola stared down at the soft carpet of cloud already thousands of feet below them. It seemed to extend for ever, sealing the world and its darkness away from this towering height.

'We're travelling at just under the speed of sound,' César informed her casually. 'Six hundred and ten knots, to be precise.' By his expression, he was relishing her mixture of terror and excitement. 'She isn't designed for supersonic flight, but we're planning a Mark II version that will be.'

'My God,' Lola said, shaking her head, 'the very *ultimate* status-symbol!'

'Oh, it's more than that. Sub-sonic flight is noisier, bumpier, and much less efficient. Travelling faster than sound is an incredibly peaceful experience, believe me.'

'I do,' she said, beginning to catch her breath at last, 'I do.' Her brother was going to be green with envy when she told him about *this*. What would her family make of this extraordinary man, who had achieved so much, so early in life? No one in their experience had ever been like César Levertov. Would they find him unapproachable, over-awing? No, she decided instinctively. César had too much warmth in him, too much kindness, to over-awe Tom or her father. She could easily see Tom, though, getting a bad case of hero-worship!

César guided the plane slowly down towards the cloud-layer again, until the tumbled white heaps seemed to be sweeping past only a few feet beneath the fuselage. The canopy was flooded with sun, and Lola relaxed for the first time, lolling her head back against the leather to revel in the sheer sensual pleasure of the experience. The sunlight splashed on the golden skin of her arms and legs was warm, almost hot.

'Where are we heading?' Mamie demanded from behind.

'Out to sea at the moment,' César called back. 'There's nothing but cloud inland. Look!' Even as he spoke, the clouds were beginning to give way, revealing a glittering cobalt sea beneath them. Mrs Prenderghast gingerly unbuckled herself, and came forward to the flight-deck to stare out of the windows at the exhilarating view ahead.

'This is a fantastic experience,' she assured them, staring at the tiny fleet of fishing-boats that was now in view far below.

'I won't show you any aerobatics,' César smiled, 'but you can see how manoeuvrable she is.' He looked at Mamie with a twinkle. 'Care to order one?'

'What do they cost?' Mamie demanded practically.

'Surprisingly little. Less than two or three Rolls

Royces, anyway.' He took the jet in another long
sweep, the sun flashing off its wings, so that they
were flying parallel to the cloudbank. The tiny
white triangle of a yacht swept far beneath them.
Henri had slid a cocktail cabinet from behind a
walnut-veneered panel, and Lola grinned at
Mamie's expression as he offered her a perfectly
made daiquiri. Lola left the cockpit space to César
and her employer, and went aft to study the
passenger area. The sensation of speed was more
muted in the plush lounge, but no amount of
interior luxury could ever fully disguise the
thrusting, raw power of this aircraft. Yes, the
Churchill was going to sell very well indeed.

The flight lasted a bare ten minutes before César
turned the jet's nose back towards Antibes. As
they ploughed down through the thick white
clouds, Lola was staring ahead dreamily. Flying,
she had just discovered, could be one of the most
deliciously sensual experiences of all. . .

Lola's mind was whirling with impressions of
the day when they got back to the hotel. César
Levertov had stirred some very deep currents
within her. Even now, those currents were still
moving, as though everything inside her was being
rearranged, shifted around. As though everything
were making room for something which had been
missing for years.

Despite her beauty, and her warm, romantic
nature, Lola had never had a deep relationship
with any man.

Throughout her university years she'd had the
deep inner dream that she would meet someone
one day—a shadowy male figure of her imagination, someone who would share her interests, be
gentle and loving with her, stir her heart and make

all her wishes come true. Someone real she could look up to and love.

That dream hadn't materialised.

Oh, there had been men eager to take her out, one or two she'd even grown quite fond of, and still corresponded with; but no one who fitted that shadowy dream-image which had been so close to her heart, yet which she so seldom dared even think of. No one had possessed the intelligence, the strength, the *specialness* which she'd always imagined would one day set her heart on fire.

And she'd found herself in the slightly disoriented position of having several boyfriends whose company she enjoyed, yet none she really cared about. Even the one or two who really had been special, and who had set her heart racing with hope at first, had swiftly proved to be vague, slightly bitter disappointments.

All that, of course, had been in the aftermath of her mother's death, and she had admittedly been stunned and withdrawn for several months after the rainy funeral. Her mother's death had hit her hard, and not even Tom or her father had been able to bring her out of her melancholy for a long, long while. Maybe her emotions had simply been overshadowed by the tragedy.

That emotional barrier inside her was what made César all the more special to her. He didn't just excite her intellectually; there was a warmth in him, a sexuality which called to her deeply and strongly. For him, the barrier didn't even exist.

She remembered young men who'd called her cold and unresponsive. They'd spoken about 'commitments' and the importance of sex in loving relationships—as though they were blind to the fact that the lovely blonde with the misty grey-green eyes simply didn't *want* to be committed, was not and never could be in love with them.

There had been a time, during her third year, when she'd begun to wonder whether she was indeed emotionally frigid. She'd even considered the idea of going to see a woman psychologist with whom she'd been vaguely friendly; but somehow, it was too important, too intimate a subject for her to bring out, and she'd never made it to the plush, though book-lined office.

She stared out at the blue skies and palm-lined avenues of Nice, unseeing. What César was doing to her had never happened before. It had been as though he'd swept away her timid, shadowy dream-image—and sent a blaze of vivid sunlight into the darkest and most inward corners of her soul.

Was she overreacting wildly to a casually bestowed interest from a very attractive man? She smiled slightly as she climbed into her bath, and closed her eyes to summon up César's face again. Maybe she was. But at least he'd proved that there was, somewhere inside her, a profound reservoir of emotion that could be stirred.

It was still raining the next day, Saturday. Lola encountered Mr Akhtopol in the foyer, looking very much the East European in a drab black mackintosh, as she scurried in from the downpour late in the afternoon. She'd been out for a breath of air, and he was obviously on his way somewhere in a hurry. There was someone with him, a burly man whose dusky face was pock-marked, as though he'd had smallpox long ago. He walked with an odd, slouching gait which contrasted almost grotesquely with Akhtopol's brisk waddle. Akhtopol shot her one of his suspicious glances, but she hardly had time to feel any tension at the encounter before he'd clamped his hat down and hurried out into the rain with his companion. She turned to look back after the two slightly sinister figures as she furled her dripping umbrella. The other man's eyes had been small, black, and somehow hot. Cruel eyes that gave Lola an uncomfortable feeling down her spine.

The flight in the Churchill yesterday had given her a much sharper insight into the reasons that would prompt Mr Akhtopol to bribe someone for the design blueprints. The airplane was bound to represent a serious threat to other manufacturers in the light-aircraft industry, and would be in any case a prize well worth risking much for. Her mind's eye still held the picture of the Churchill gleaming in its hangar, the sweeping wings poised for flight.

The two bulky bodies disappeared into the doors of a taxi, and Lola took the lift up to their apartment.

She found she was humming under breath. A tiny detail—but she couldn't remember having hummed a tune in absolute years. Since that afternoon at the Baroness's, her mood had changed in direct contrast to the darkening weather. Of that boredom and depression that had been haunting her all along on this trip, nothing now remained. Suddenly, she felt that she really was twenty-two, and not a hundred and ten! Life was full of magic, full of infinite possibilities. There was a potential adventure lurking in every moment, Bulgarian spies and dazzling part-Russian industrialists peopling this summer landscape—and above all, the hint of love in the air!

There was a note waiting for her in the suite. *'Have gone to the cocktail lounge with Vivien Roche,'* it read. *'Join us if you feel like it—will be there till dinner—MP.'* Lola folded the note up, thinking that there were few things she would rather *not* do than join Mrs Prenderghast for daiquiris at that moment. She walked to the window, and stared down at the rainy streets far below. Should she 'phone César? He had given her his number, and she ached for the sound of his voice.

Yes. But first a change of her rain-spattered clothes, and a quick, hot bath. She'd put on a neutral grey jumper and jeans that hugged her elegantly slender hips and thighs for her excursion, and somehow when she spoke to César she wanted to be in a silk dressing-gown!

Suddenly, though, a thought made her eyes widen. The Bulgarian was out. And their balcony adjoined his.

Could she possibly get across, and into the suite next door? The thought that the vital computer-tape might be in there, lying on a table, tantalised her.

She walked quickly out on to the balcony, oblivious to the rain that spattered her face. The partition between the balconies was high, and obstructed with racks of lush pot-plants, but she felt sure she'd be able to scramble over it—with a bit of luck. Excitement ignited inside her. If he had left the balcony door unlocked—or if her own key also fitted that lock—

Did she dare? Not for anyone in the world except César! Impulsively, she pulled the key from their own door, thrust it into her jeans pocket, and started shifting the plants away from the adjoining wall.

If Akhtopol hadn't disposed of the tape, and if it was still somewhere in his apartment, she might yet be able to save César's design from Cirrus. Panting, she heaved a massive planter aside, and surveyed the wall. It was over ten feet high, but there must be something on the other side, because the Bulgarian had been able to peer over the wall at Mrs Prenderghast. Her white leather peep-toe sandals with their fashionably low heels weren't ideal for the job, but she didn't want to waste time changing them. Standing on the edge of the cast-iron planter, she reached up as far as she could. Two feet short.

She scrambled down, and looked around. There was a large wooden tub with a spiky cordiline growing in it. She hefted it precariously on to the corner of the planter, and stood on top of that. It wobbled nastily under her feet, and the sharp leaves stabbed her calves through the denim, but she got her fingers over the top of the wall this time, and hauled herself desperately up, hearing the muscles crack in her shoulders. The pot thudded to the ground below her, spilling soil over the pristine tiles. For a horrible second or two she dangled there, thinking she was going to slip back, but then she managed to get one knee on the top, and heaved herself painfully on to the narrow ledge.

She peered gingerly down.

It was a horribly sheer drop down to her right, and the crawling toy cars made her mind reel for a moment with vertigo. And worse, the floor on the other side was bare. Damn! It was a long drop on to the stone tiles. The Bulgarian must have dragged something over to stand on. Gritting her teeth, Lola swung her long legs over the top of the wall, and lowered herself on protesting arms.

It suddenly occurred to her that although Akhtopol himself was out, there just might be someone else in the Bulgarian's apartment.

Damn! Why the hell hadn't she thought to knock and find out? It was too late now; she couldn't support her weight any longer, and she slid downwards, scraping her back on the rustic-design bricks, and landed with a bone-jarring slap of leather heels on the Bulgarian's balcony.

She crouched there, waiting. Being on someone else's territory was a distinctly peculiar feeling. Her heart pounded unpleasantly against her ribs, and she thought wryly that she'd never have made as fluent a burglar as César. She was half-expecting a shout or an indignant face at the window, but neither came. Cautiously, she edged to the window, and peered through. The suite seemed similar to the one she'd just left, though slightly smaller, and it was apparently deserted.

She tip-toed to the balcony door, and tried the handle. It was locked. A cold feeling drifted across her heart. She wasn't an Olympic mountaineer, like César. If she couldn't get in this way, she was simply going to have to sit out here on the balcony until the Bulgarian returned. The sensation of having trapped herself was not pleasant. Biting her lip, she pulled the key out of her pocket, and pushed it into the keyhole. Her heart sank as it refused to turn. It was a different lock. She might have known! She twisted as hard as she could, and felt some give this time. Then, with a startlingly loud snap, the lock clicked open.

She hesitated for a breathless second, then pushed the door open.

The suite was dark, and in some disorder. A half-eaten meal lay on a tray on the floor, in front of the television screen. The coffee-table was piled with newspapers in French, German, and what Lola guessed must be Bulgarian. Aviation magazines were scattered on the couches.

At the other end of the room, a writing-table was covered in notes and calculations, and a portable computer had been set up on a stool beside it. Her university experience told her that it was a model that used flat disks, not reels, and she didn't waste time checking there.

Moving as silently as she could, she went through to the bedroom. The bed was unmade, and she caught the acrid rosewater-and-scent smell of the Bulgarian's body. She wrinkled her pert nose. It stayed wrinkled as she surveyed the expensive but soiled clothes piled on a chair, the porno magazine lying open on the floor, the bottle of aspirins which had been spilled and not picked up.

Mr Akhtopol was a slob. A lonely slob.

And being in this apartment was making her feel horribly like a voyeur. She spotted the black briefcase standing on the far side of the bed, and went to it instinctively. It was locked, with hefty-looking twin brass locks. Without thinking, she pulled open the bedside cabinet drawer, and rummaged through it shamelessly. Underneath the passport, two slim keys in a flat leather holder.

Her hands were shaking as she tried the locks, and found that they opened.

The contents of the briefcase, unlike the suite, were arranged in ultra-neat order. In the centre compartment was a flat plastic box about fourteen inches square, marked with the logo of a famous computer company. She fumbled it open excitedly. Inside was a futuristic-looking tape-reel, made out of some aluminium alloy. The matt black tape told her nothing, and on the hub of the reel were only a set of complicated serial numbers.

She snapped the box shut. It *had* to be César's tape! Her heart soared as she imagined the light in those golden eyes for a second—and then sudden terror that she would be caught brought panic dangerously close. All she wanted was to get out of this suite, now, *fast*!

She had to force herself to lock the briefcase, put it back where it had stood and slip the keys back in the drawer. She ran to the balcony door, her mouth dry.

Damn! How was she going to get back over the wall? The writing-table? No, of course not. He would see it there, and know which way the thief had come.

Thief? That's right, she told herself grimly, that's what you are now. So *think*.

The only way out was through the front door. She closed the balcony door carefully, and tried to lock it with her key. This time, the key wouldn't shift at all, though her knuckles were white with the strain. Having clicked one way, it was obviously not going to click back. Cursing under her breath, Lola pocketed the key, and ran for the front door. Maybe he would forget whether he'd locked the door or not. Maybe.

She slipped the tape under her jumper, and feeling the guilty coldness against her skin, opened the mahogany door, and peeped nervously into the corridor. It was deserted. She slipped through, closed the door behind her, and stood under the soft light, panting as fast as though she'd just run a mile in record time.

She was locked out of her own suite now. No matter—she had to get to César immediately. She found a few coins in her pocket, and ran to the lift.

'Come on, come *on*,' she heard herself muttering as the lift whooshed steadily down. Her nerves were ready to jump out of her skin. The mixture of guilt and exhilaration was making her nauseous, too. Dear God, she must have been mad! She'd just committed an unmitigated crime back there. If she were to see the black, bulky figure of Mr Akhtopol now, she knew she'd scream.

In the foyer she slipped into one of the payphone booths, the tape still clutched against her flat stomach. She peered through the perspex windows, but no one seemed to have noticed her guilty behaviour. Quickly, she dialled César's number, holding the coin at the ready. She squeezed her eyes shut, praying, as the burrs sounded.

His warm, calm voice broke into the sterile sound like a benediction, and she rammed the coin home.

'César! It's me. Listen, can you come round to the hotel immediately?'

'Is anything wrong?' His voice was alert.

'No. I mean *yes*. I've stolen your tape back from Mr Akhtopol.'

'You've done *what*?' Amusement struggled with disbelief in his voice, and came up half-angry. 'You maniac! How? No—don't tell me. Are you in the suite?'

'In the foyer, downstairs. In one of the payphones.'

'I'll be there in thirty minutes. Go into the

ladies' toilet, Lola, and don't come out until five-forty-five. I'll be waiting at reception. Got that?'

'Yes,' she said breathlessly.

'And Lola——'

'Yes?'

'Don't go away.'

It was still raining as she ran across the street with him, her hand clutched in his, and piled into the car he'd left purring in an illegal parking-zone. Once inside, he pulled her close and kissed her once, hard.

'Now,' he said, holding her away from him to study her face with concerned eyes, 'what in God's name have you been getting up to?'

She tugged the tape out from under her jumper, and rapidly spilled her story out while he studied the serial numbers thoughtfully. He glanced up, tight-lipped as she described how she'd clambered over the balcony, but didn't interrupt until she'd finished.

'—and that's what happened,' she concluded, rather anxious at his forbidding expression. She didn't tell him that she hadn't been able to lock the balcony door after her—by the look on his face, he wouldn't be amused at *that* little detail. 'Is it the right tape?'

'I don't know,' he admitted, turning it over in his hands. 'Poincarré made the copy, and only he would know.' He passed it back to her, his mouth becoming grim. 'You've been a crazy little fool, Lola. What if you'd slipped off the balcony? Or if he'd come back and caught you there? God in heaven, girl—you might have been killed, and all for the sake of a few diagrams!'

'I just didn't think,' she replied truthfully, rather

hurt by his lack of gratitude. 'I just saw a chance to get your tape back . . .' She studied his face nervously. 'You're not really angry with me?'

'Damn right I'm angry,' he snapped, gold flaming in his eyes. His fingers brushed roughly through her hair, and tugged ruthlessly hard. 'If I'd known what insane tricks you were getting up to——' His expression gentled as he took in the remorse in her pale face. 'Oh, hell . . . I can't be angry, Lola, no. Not when you look like that. But for the love of God, don't risk your life like that again. Okay?'

'Okay,' she nodded, his concern going to her head like wine. He really cared!

'One burglar in any relationship is enough,' he warned. 'Don't you *ever* do anything like that again.' His eyes were golden-warm as he brushed her damp hair out of her eyes. 'Thank you for doing it, *ma petite*. For doing it for my sake.' He kissed her again, his lips velvety against hers; but as the kiss ignited into the bone-melting passion they'd both experienced before, he pushed her firmly back into her seat, and looped the safety-belt around her. 'I'm afraid we're going to have to postpone the rest of that kiss for a while. We'd better get your booty to a computer quickly, little one—if possible, before our friend Mr Akhtopol gets back.'

He put his foot down, and the car surged forward into the traffic. Feeling suddenly wonderful, Lola snuggled back against the leather seat. 'Where are we going?' she asked, her terror at last beginning to give way to pleasurable excitement. She never felt safer than with César.

'Home.' He smiled at her briefly. 'St Jean-Cap-Ferrat. We could go to the factory, but it's unnecessary. I play with aerodynamic ideas in my spare time—and that means computers. I use a Starbrain which will take that size tape.'

'Wouldn't it be wonderful if this *were* the copy of your design!' she said, grey-green eyes bright.

'More than wonderful,' he agreed. A dry expression crossed the mobile mouth. 'But don't put too much faith in it, Lola. Big businesses run on tapes like this, and it could just as easily be something like a list of last year's wage-rises at Cirrus.'

She nodded at his warning, and glanced at her watch. Nearly six. Dinner began at seven, and she hadn't left any sort of note for Mamie. Never mind—exceptional cases called for exceptional measures! She would explain all when she got back.

César drove fast, well over the legal limit, and the sleek car responded with a roar of perfectly tuned engines. Within a few minutes they were out of Nice, and in the fast lane of the autoroute towards Villefranche and Beaulieu.

He dropped down a gear as they came off the motorway exit, and made for the little promontory of Cap-Ferrat. The evening sky was clearing now, and the village was charming in the cool, rain-washed light. The Mediterranean beyond was as calm and lovely as a sea of lapis-lazuli. Lola couldn't help her sigh of delight. Sights like this confirmed why the Côte d'Azur remained one of the most magnetic tourist-attractions of them all.

'I live on the seafront,' he told her. 'Logically, I should live in Nice, I suppose, at the centre of all the business and fashion. Unfortunately, being fashionable bores me stiff. So I decided to build here because of the peace and the solitude.' He swung the car into a short, palm-lined driveway. 'Here it is.'

Lola stared at the house, spellbound. It was a long, low, ultra-modern structure built on the very edge of the twenty-foot cliff that overlooked the sea. The low-profile design echoed the peaceful landscape beautifully, and a garden of mature trees and shrubs helped to blend the white walls into the rocky, almost African shoreline. César parked the space-age Lamborghini, the same classic white as the house, in front of a wide patio that would be bliss in hot weather, and which was now wet and empty. At the side the Mediterranean creamed softly twenty feet below the huge, tinted glass wall that made up almost the whole front of the villa. She followed him, open-mouthed through the door into the house. The interior was airy, composed with crisp, clean whites and greys. Nothing fussy or overstated. The impression of light and space was delicious.

'You designed this place yourself,' she guessed, stunned by the unique design of the place.

'Five years ago,' he nodded. His amber eyes watched her reactions intently. 'Do you like it?'

'It's——' She hesitated, turning round in the tranquil space of the living-room. The bronze-tinted glass cast a delightfully warm light over the room. In the dazzling sunlight of a South of France summer, she knew, the bronzed windows would make the interior of the house a sea of liquid gold. 'It's very, very beautiful!'

'I'm glad you approve,' he smiled. 'People seem to react strongly—either love or hate at first sight.'

People? she thought with a stab of jealousy. How many beautiful women had he brought here over the years? She walked to the vast window.

'I've never seen anything like this. What happens in storms?' she wanted to know.

'That glass is the same stuff I use in my cockpits,' he said, coming to join her at the window. 'It's thermo-retaining—very warm—and reflective from the outside.' He took a heavy stone ashtray from a table, and swung it hard at the glass. Lola gasped in horror, but instead of a horrible crash, there was only a firm thud as the ashtray rebounded in his hand. She leaned forward, wide-eyed. The window was utterly unmarked. He watched her face, amused at her alarm. 'It's practically indestructible, especially when it's two inches thick, as this is. Formidably expensive—but it should never need repair or painting, and that will make it very economical in the long run. Maybe all houses will be built like this one day. As for storms—it's like being 20,000 leagues under the sea, then. Sometimes in winter the waves actually smash against the glass. You can't hear them. But some people find it hair-raising.'

'And you?'

'I love it,' he admitted frankly. 'I love storms. I love to see the sea and the sky in all their moods. That's partly why I built the house here on the shore, and why I made this out of glass. There's nothing quite as exhilarating as seeing the waves crash on to the glass.' Their eyes met, amber-gold probing soft green. 'You think I'm crazy?'

'No.' She was acutely aware of the proud, untameable force in him, like some storm-winged albatross, revelling in tempest and adversity. She could imagine him at the controls of that slim silver jet, cruising high above mortal worries and mundanity . . .

She turned away, her mouth suddenly dry. 'No, I don't think you're crazy.' He was almost incredibly desirable, lean and hard despite the elegant silk shirt and dark jeans, so utterly male, so utterly authoritative.

He walked to the side wall, smiling, and slid a burr walnut panel aside. Behind it was revealed the gleaming face of a big computer, three screens staring blankly out in a row. She watched as he slotted the aluminium disk into place, looped the tape on to the take-up reel, and set the machine whirring. He turned to her as the lights began to wink.

'The programme's loading now. It'll take just a few minutes more.' The magnificent face eased into a quiet smile. 'Don't stand there looking so lost and shy. What's making you so nervous?'

'All this,' she confessed. 'It's a bit—overwhelming, I'm afraid.'

'Overwhelming,' he repeated. 'You don't include me in that, I hope?' His voice was a deep caress, and she smiled tentatively.

'No.'

He walked over to her, moving with the grace of a panther, and slid his arms round her waist. 'Good. The only place I want to overwhelm you is in bed.' She felt herself colouring. Sometimes she wished he wouldn't say things like that. He made her feel so helpless! She was burningly conscious of his hard, flat midriff through the silk, his hips uncompromisingly taut against hers. 'Otherwise, my love, you're much too independent a spirit to be overwhelmed by anything.' He kissed her lightly on the mouth, his mouth amused, warm, then released her. 'You don't deserve a drink after all your wickedness, but I'm going to take pity on you. A brandy?'

She nodded, feeling breathless. Touching him, kissing him, always left her feeling as though she'd already drunk some potent, fiery liquor! He poured her a brandy, and she sat down with it in the beautifully comfortable white hide sofa that was the focus of this end of the room. She glanced round as he made some adjustments to the computer.

Beautiful. The entire house was marked by a powerful, uncompromising taste. The harmony of the room came not through kitschy decor and matching colour-schemes, but through the dominant mind that had chosen all the varied and fascinating things in it. Like the mixture of old and new paintings, the modern ceramics and the glass shelves of softly illuminated seashells, the abundance of healthy green plants, the marble busts— and above all, the ultramarine vastness of the sea, which had been allowed to participate so strongly in the mood of the house. Oddly, though, the house wasn't ship-like at all; it gave an impression of great stability, perhaps because of all the strong verticals and horizontals in it.

César was lowering fine wicker blinds over the huge window. The computer screens were now each reading one word—READY. He switched on a single softly glowing lamp, and settled down on the sofa beside her, stretching out his long legs comfortably.

'Now—let's see what we've got here.' He was holding a remote-control console in his hand, and he punched some buttons on it. The screens flickered into movement. A stream of figures and calculations began buzzing vertically by. She couldn't make much sense of them, and she sat with bated breath, waiting for his reaction.

He keyed the console again, and the screens flicked to a different set of figures, interlarded with brief snatches of text.

'Sales figures,' he said shortly. 'And some kind of analysis. Tapes like these are rather like big books,' he informed her, 'only more complicated in the way the pages are arranged. At the moment we're electronically flipping through the pages, so to speak.'

Suddenly a series of complicated diagrams began appearing on the screen.

'There!' Lola said excitedly. He stopped the text, and studied the designs intently for a few moments, then shook his head.

'Not mine, I'm afraid. Something much smaller than the Churchill.' He keyed successive aspects of the diagram on to the screen, his intelligent, alert gaze locked on the glowing green lines. 'A satellite. Even a guided missile, perhaps. Not from my factory.' Lola slumped back in the sofa, feeling disappointment wash coldly over her. It looked as if it was turning out that all her effort had been for nothing. She'd so wanted to make it all right for him. . .

They sat in silence as page after page of unrelieved text flashed by—figures, figures, figures.

'It's not the right tape, is it?' she asked mournfully at last. He shook his head gently.

'It doesn't seem to be. These are all business deals that Mr Akhtopol has concluded in the past year—or hopes to conclude while he's at the airshow.' César studied some individual pages. 'For example, here he sells some cargo planes to a Saudi oil-company. This next thing is the text of an agreement with RKM, another big aviation company.' More text scrolled past. 'Here he's hoping to make a deal with BP to supply them with helicopters for an offshore rig . . .' He keyed more instructions into the console, and the figures blurred past. 'Let's move towards the end of the tape. Now then—here are more orders he hopes to get. Components for Alitalia. More helicopters, this time for the Belgian traffic police. Mr Akhtopol seems to be a high-class travelling salesman, Lola—and this is his order-book. And I'm afraid it's nothing more than that.' He glanced at her woebegone expression, and smiled gently. 'My poor baby—and after all your adventures. Are you very disappointed?'

'Yes,' she said in a choky voice, close to crying. She'd been so convinced that this was the stolen tape, and without being aware of it, she'd set her heart on seeing César's delight at getting it back.

He stood up, switched the computer off, and came beside her to take her in his arms.

'Never mind, brave little one.' His arms were infinitely comforting around her, and she laid her head against his chest dreamily, her eyes misty with tears. 'You did wonderfully to get it,' he said softly, his breath warm in her hair. 'It could so easily have been the right tape. We'll have to be content with that. Yes?'

'Yes,' she smiled blurrily.

He caressed her cheek. 'I'll get the tape back to Akhtopol tomorrow sometime, so don't worry about that. But I'm truly sorry you went through that ordeal for nothing. Were you terrified?'

'Out of my wits,' she confessed ruefully. 'But it was too late by then. I don't know what came over me—some temporary madness, I guess.'

'You thought that if I could do it, then so could you?'

'Something like that,' she said wryly. She looked up at him. 'But I don't regret doing it, César, not for one second. I wanted to help, to do something for you.'

'You did.' The dark strength of his face was lit by a smile. 'I find it astounding that you risked so much for me, knowing so little about me. Astounding—and a little humbling.' He kissed the corners of her mouth gently, lingeringly. 'Do I really mean that much to you, Lola?' She didn't answer, her heart thudding at the intimate caress of his mouth. 'Well,' he smiled quietly, 'you mean a lot to me, my little burglar.' He kissed her again, a slow mutual exploration that sent hot quicksilver through her veins. She whispered his name, clinging to the power of his shoulders as their kiss deepened into tenderness. She couldn't stop her own body from arching against him in a wave of longing. This ache she felt for him was piercing, incredibly powerful despite all the tinkling bells of common sense that warned her it was too soon to feel like this. She knew she ought to stop this, now, before it was too late—but the searing command of his mouth was irresistible; it exactly matched her own swelling desire to be commanded, to surrender utterly to him.

His eyes were dreamily narrowed with passion as he kissed her throat, his lips brushing the scented hollows of her collarbone.

Nothing mattered any more, not Mamie nor Mr Akhtopol nor the Churchill plans. César's fingers traced the lines of her face wonderingly—almost, she thought dizzily, as though she were a work of art he couldn't quite believe.

'What are you looking at?' she whispered, trying to sound light.

'*Ma chérie,*' he murmured huskily, smiling down at her. 'If you knew how very beautiful you were ... And your mouth is so soft, as though it had never kissed a man before.'

'Is that a polite way of telling me I'm amateurish?' she said, answering his smile.

'It's a polite way of telling you you're very desirable.' He drew her arms round him. 'Hold me,' he commanded huskily, his mouth claiming hers with gentle authority. Their kiss was now lingering, a dreamy, delicious union that was like sweet music. With a lack of shame that she could never have imagined, she slid her hands under César's shirt, running them over the swelling muscles of his back. The strength of his body was almost frightening, even though she knew she could trust his steely control over that hard power.

She felt him unfasten her shirt, and shuddered as his fingers drew lines of fire across her silky skin. When his caress reached the curves of her breasts, it was with a sweet physical shock that took the breath from her lungs in a gasp. His touch was unbelievably tender, a slow exploration of her femininity that drove her to the edge of her control. It was as though all that long waiting had sharpened her senses, as though her whole life had been a preparation for this relationship, the exaltation of this man's touch and kiss.

Her delicate skin was almost unbearably sensitive to his touch—and by his gentleness she knew he was instinctively aware of that. The satiny tips of her breasts grew tense and full against his stroking palms, until she cried out helplessly against his mouth.

Her body seemed to be melting, flowing like warm honey with his. When she could bear no more, he seemed to know instinctively, and he held her tight in his arms, crushing her against him in the dreamy silence.

'You're too wonderful to be true,' he said huskily.

'César,' she whispered, answering a question he had asked an eternity ago, 'you'll never know just how much you mean to me . . .'

'Then I hope one day you'll try and show me,' he said quietly. She smiled against his chest, despite her ache for him, and wondered dreamily what was going to become of this strange, marvellous, almost unreal relationship . . .

It seemed like an age that she lay there, her senses filled with him, the touch of him, his warmth and the musky smell of his body. Then, slowly, he released her, and brushed the tumbled gold of her hair out of her eyes, studying the beautiful oval face as though it were the first he'd ever seen. 'Lola. Such a lovely name, like a mouthful of red wine.'

She smiled shakily in return. 'César . . . it suits you. Imperious and commanding.'

'Indeed.' He stroked her cheek, shaking his head. 'You do fantastic things to me, Lola.'

'And you to me,' she nodded, wondering whether he really had any inkling of the forest-fire he'd ignited inside her.

'I'm glad to hear it,' he purred. 'Now do you believe me that there is something special between us?'

She took his big, bronzed hand in both her own, and stared down at it. 'I didn't want to at first,' she said quietly. 'It seemed almost too fantastic to be true. Yes, César. I do believe you.'

CHAPTER FIVE

THE Bulgarian monster's guttural voice echoed through Lola's dreams.

'I hov been robbed,' he was roaring. 'Thieves! Thieves!'

She sat up, blinking stupidly. She'd barely had five hours' sleep since César had driven her back to the hotel last night, and yesterday had been a long and highly emotional day. She wasn't exactly feeling bright.

But it was no nightmare. She could quite distinctly hear Mr Akhtopol's roar in the corridor outside. And she could also hear the nervous tones of the balding manager, apparently trying to placate him.

'*Non, non!*' Mr Akhtopol interrupted, '*ce n'est pas une erreur!* Valuable things, priceless things hov been stolen from me!'

Lola felt foreboding sweep coldly over her, and clambered out of bed. It was seven-thirty, and she could hear Mrs Prenderghast cursing in her bed at having been awakened by the noise. Apparently Mr Akhtopol had just discovered the loss of his tape. The incidents of yesterday, culminating in the flaring passion of last night, flashed vividly through her mind. She pulled on her dressing-gown and tip-toed through the drawing-room to the door, and listened at it. Mr Akhtopol was stamping up and down the corridor. She could hear the heavy tread of his shoes.

'But Monsieur Akhtopol,' the manager was saying nervously, 'you cannot accuse a fellow-guest like this——'

'It was her, yes! Her, I say. I hov proof!'

'But surely Mrs Prenderghast——'

'Not Mrs Prenderghast,' the Bulgarian snarled in scorn. Something—probably his fist—crashed against the door, and Lola jumped a foot. 'The young one, the one with the yellow hair——'

'Miss Golightly?' the manager asked incredulously. 'That is not possible.'

'Not possible, pah! I hov *proof*,' Mr Akhtopol repeated belligerently. Lola's heart sank to her bare soles. He had obviously noticed the unlocked balcony door.

'Oh, damn,' she whispered. Her instinct was to telephone César at once, but she was forced to dismiss that idea. Involving him wouldn't help in the slightest now. What the hell was she going to do?

'Is it that wretched monster again?' Mrs Prenderghast demanded, stalking out of her bedroom in a memorable violet-and-green bathrobe.

'Yes, Mrs Prenderghast,' Lola said miserably.

'Rot the man,' Mrs Prenderghast snapped. 'I'm beginning to hate Nice. And where were *you* until one o'clock this morning, I'd like to know?' Without waiting for an answer, she flung open the door of the suite.

The Bulgarian was standing outside, fully dressed. His congested face spoke of considerable anger, and for once the comical side of his personality didn't seem to be in evidence to Lola. He pointed a thick forefinger like a pistol at Lola's face.

'She,' he spat out. 'She has stolen my valuable documents!'

'How dare you?' Mrs Prenderghast said, beginning to quiver with outrage.

'I am desolate, Madame,' the little manager said, trying to interpose himself between the two. He looked more than ever the hunted minnow, but Lola wasn't in the mood for smiles just then. Akhtopol looked murderous. 'An unfortunate confusion, alas. Monsieur Akhtopol appears to have lost——'

'Not lost,' Mr Akhtopol growled. 'Stolen.' His black eyes bored into Lola's with such hatred that she took an involuntary step backwards. She'd never seen such anger in a human face before. 'And you hov stolen it, Mademoiselle.'

'What utter nonsense!' Mrs Prenderghast's face was mottled with indignation. 'You watch what you're saying, my man, or you'll find yourself in court for defamation!'

'Do not interfere, old woman,' Akhtopol rasped. With contemptuous ease, he thrust the half-open door aside, and advanced on Lola. 'Where is it, little thief? Give it to me!'

'I d-don't know what you're talking about,' Lola stammered, backing away from him. She was trying not to show it, but she was really frightened of him; there was an aura of violence about him that appalled her. Perhaps she should have called César after all!

'Of course you know,' he rasped. She shook her head frantically, feeling horribly vulnerable in her flimsy gown with precious little else on underneath. The little manager scuttled in after the Bulgarian, trying to placate Mrs Prenderghast's gobblings of fury on the one hand while he restrained Akhtopol on the other.

'Monsieur, please—consider your position! Surely some mistake has been made that can be easily rectified——'

'Mistake?' Akhtopol swung on him with snarling lips, then glanced at the balcony door. He yanked the drapes aside, and flung the door open. He thrust his large, football-shaped head out, then turned to them with triumph gleaming in his eyes. 'Aha! I suppose this is also a mistake?'

They followed his accusing finger. Lola stared in horror at the partition. Why in God's name hadn't she cleared up the mess before going to sleep last night? The plants pushed to one side, the tumbled wooden tub, the soil scattered on the tiles—and her own neat footprints glaringly evident in the rain-dampened soil. Damning evidence.

'What can you say now?' the Bulgarian demanded savagely. Mrs Prenderghast and the manager stared from the mess to Lola in silent astonishment. Now was the time she should deny all knowledge, look amazed—but she couldn't do it. She'd never been able to lie, and burgling Mr Akhtopol's apartment was the most criminal thing she'd ever done in her life. She could no more have hidden her guilt than she could have denied that the sun was shining—which it was doing, very brightly, upon the evidence of her crime.

'I can't say anything,' she replied quietly.

'*Mademoiselle!*' the manager said, more pleading than commanding, 'can you explain this?'

She shook her head. It was soon going to be time, it seemed, to face the music!

'She can say nothing,' the Bulgarian snarled, 'because it is she who has stolen my property— look at her footprint!' He swung round to face Lola. 'Give it back to me!' Lola could only shake

her head. César had promised to get the tape back
to Akhtopol today sometime—but what to do
until then? Hold her peace, and hope that the
ordeal went by quickly? It was beginning to dawn
on her that she had been very stupid indeed in not
telling César about the clues as to her identity she
had so clumsily left behind. Had she done so, he
would have found some way of avoiding this
inevitable detection.

'*Mademoiselle*——' the manager begged, his
eyes imploring. Lola could only hang her head,
feeling very close to tears. With a Gallic shrug of
unhappy resignation, the manager turned to Mrs
Prenderghast, 'I am very much afraid this is
becoming a matter for the police.'

'Poliss?' the Bulgarian repeated, his brows
coming down like thunder. 'Not necessary.' He
gripped Lola's elbows painfully hard, and glared
into her face. 'Pliss to give me ten minutes alone
with this woman. Soon I will have the truth. I
guarantee it.'

'There's no question of that, Monsieur,' the
manager said quietly, cutting through Mrs
Prenderghast's protests, and pushing the Bulgarian
away from Lola.

'Then I insist you allow me to search this
apartment,' he demanded. 'It must be here, my
computer-tape.'

'That is also impossible, Monsieur Akhtopol,'
the manager said firmly. A kind of sad dignity
seemed to have settled on his diminutive shoulders. He turned to Lola. 'Please,' he said in a
low voice, 'if you know anything about this
business, anything at all, tell me now. For your
sake.'

'There's nothing I can say, Monsieur,' she

repeated gently. The man's honest face was a
burning reproach to her. She had never felt so
horribly guilty in all her life, and having to deceive
everyone even further was an impossible order.
Dignified silence was her only course.

The manager's intelligent eyes were thoughtful.
'This is all very strange. It was just over a week
ago that Mademoiselle Golightly said she saw a
burglar in this apartment. We paid her no
attention then. Perhaps we should have believed
her after all.'

'She is the burglar,' Akhtopol snapped. 'All that
was nonsense to cover the truth. She is industrial
spy! The document she has taken contains
classified information about my company!' He was
gnawing his lip, a heavy agitation mingling with
his anger now. It occurred to Lola dimly that he
was making a great deal of fuss over what was
little more than a lost order-book. Surely he could
get a copy sent out to him within a few hours? 'A
minute——' the Bulgarian pleaded, knotting his
massive hands. 'I could hov it out of her in one
minute!'

Mrs Prenderghast moved protectively between
him and Lola, her beaky face determined. 'You lay
a finger on her,' she promised grimly, fists on her
massive hips, 'and I'll scratch your eyes out.'

'I have a friend in the Sûreté nationale,' the
manager began. 'I will contact him about this
matter——'

'*No.*' The Bulgarian shook his head urgently, his
brutal face uneasy. 'There is no need for your
cursed police.'

'We have no alternative, M'sieu Akhtopol. But
first, we must examine your apartment meticu-
lously, to make sure there is no possibility of an

error. After all, the tape may possibly be still there, no?'

Akhtopol's face was twisted with anger. Abruptly he shrugged. 'Useless. But we search again, okay.' There was now a sheen of sweat on his forehead, and he was looking positively ill.

'*Bien*, M'sieu,' the manager said, taking the Bulgar by the arm, 'we go back to your apartment and look for the tape, yes? If we do not find it, I shall call my friend the Inspector. Until then—no more accusations, and no more temper, *d'accord?*' The Bulgarian shrugged, clearly forcing his passion down. But there was an almost frightened look in his eye that struck Lola as weird, considering the circumstances. '*Alors.*' The manager turned to Mrs Prenderghast. 'Please, Madame, may I request that neither you nor Mam'selle Golightly leave the apartment until this matter is cleared up?'

'I'll see to it,' Mrs Prenderghast promised, sounding tired.

'There is almost certainly some unfortunate mistake,' he went on. Unexpectedly, he reached out, and patted Lola's cold cheek with a smile. 'All will be resolved. I think I shall have one of the hotel staff wait with you——?'

'That will not be necessary,' Mrs Prenderghast said shortly. 'I shall be here with her. If Lola is indeed involved with this man's property—which I don't for a moment believe—then she must face the music. Her name has to be cleared, one way or another.' She glared at Akhtopol, her face suddenly more hostile than Lola had ever seen it. 'And if it turns out that you've accused her wrongfully, Mr Whatever-your-name-is, you'll regret this very much indeed, I guarantee it!'

The remark seemed to go right over his head. The man's furious anger seemed to be ebbing out of him almost visibly, leaving a kind of terror in its wake. He was talking to the manager in low, guttural French as they went out, obviously pleading to be allowed to do things his own way. The manager, flinty faced, merely shook his head, and led the big man out.

The door clicked shut behind them. Lola felt her lip quivering. Akhtopol's face had been truly frightened. For the first time, she was pitying the unpleasant Bulgarian. God knew what kind of trouble she'd got him into by stealing that tape, but it was obviously bad trouble! They had to get that tape back to him as quickly as possible. Mrs Prenderghast took her by the arm with surprising gentleness.

'I'm on your side, sweetie. The police will be here soon—we've only got a few minutes.' Her eyes probed Lola's. 'What's this all about?'

'I can't t-tell you,' Lola said unevenly, the concerned expression on her employer's face almost precipitating the tears that threatened.

'I have a shrewd idea——'

The shrilling of the telephone interrupted Mrs Prenderghast's sentence, and she picked it up irritably. Lola dabbed her eyes, feeling utterly wretched.

'Yes?' Mrs Prenderghast snapped. And then, in an altered voice, 'Oh—yes! I'm very well—considering the circumstances. We've just had the Bulgarian monster in here, accusing Lola of stealing some tape of his. No, he didn't touch her—she's just having a quiet cry. She's right here.' With an odd expression, Mamie held the receiver out to Lola. 'César Levertov. For you.'

Lola clutched it against her ear.

'César?'

'Are you all right?'

'I'm f-fine,' she said, smiling shakily. It was Heaven to hear him.

'How did Akhtopol know that you were the mystery burglar?' he demanded.

'I'm afraid I left some rather obvious traces at the time,' she confessed unhappily. 'I should have cleared them up, but I forgot.'

'Very clever of you,' he grated. 'Why in God's name didn't you tell me?' He didn't wait for her reply, but went on, his deep voice crackling with tension. 'Lola, I've just played that tape through again—and it's potential dynamite. You could be in a lot of danger right now. What did Akhtopol say to you?'

Briefly, she told him. 'I'm supposed to wait here with Mrs Prenderghast,' she concluded unhappily, glancing at Mamie, 'until they've searched his room. He looked terrible, César, really afraid. Is he—is he really dangerous?'

'That tape means a lot to Akhtopol, and he'll be desperate to get it back. I'll tell you the rest later,' he promised. 'There's no time now. I'm coming to get you, Lola. I'll be at the Grande in a few minutes—you stay right there in the meantime, and keep clear of Akhtopol. Understand?'

'Yes,' she nodded dazedly. 'But César, we've got to get it back to him as soon as possible!'

'Not likely,' César replied silkily. 'Have you forgotten that he's still got *my* tape? Now, can you manage to get out of your room?'

'I d-don't know.'

'You have to try. Okay?'

'I will,' she promised nervously.

'If you can get down into the foyer, slip into the tea-room on the side. That's always full, and no one will notice you there. And don't worry, I'm calling from an office just down the street from you. I'll be there in minutes.'

'I'll try,' she said again, her voice still slightly shaky.

'*Je t'aime*, Lola. You know what that means?' She closed her eyes, her throat too tight to answer. 'Okay. Put Mamie back on the line.' She obeyed, vast relief at the thought of César's imminent arrival emerging through her emotional turmoil. Mrs Prenderghast's conversation with César was monosyllabic and brief, and when she put the receiver down, her face was a picture.

'I had an idea that you were with César Levertov last night,' she said. 'And I half-suspected that this stolen tape business had something to do with you and him. Care to tell me about it?'

'I hardly know myself,' Lola said ruefully. 'I think I've been a little crazy since yesterday.'

'You *did* climb over the balcony, then—and pinch the monster's tape?' Lola nodded wryly. Mrs Prenderghast's eyes popped. 'But *why?*'

'I thought it was César's tape I was stealing.' She ran her hands through tumbled blonde hair. 'You see, Mr Akhtopol has got hold of a stolen tape belonging to César, and it was vitally important to get it back. That was why César burgled our apartment—well, he didn't know it was our apartment at the time. He thought it was Mr Akhtopol's——'

'César burgled our apartment?' Mrs Prenderghast goggled. 'César *Levertov?*' she repeated, as though there were half-a-dozen Césars involved.

'Yes. He's an expert mountaineer.' Lola drew a deep breath, realising the impossibility of explaining everything to Mrs Prenderghast in a few moments. 'It's a long story.'

'So it seems,' Mamie said, her lurid gown and staring eyes making her strangely like some exotic goldfish. 'You know, I *thought* I saw the two of you kissing on the yacht, and again at the Baroness Var's. I thought I'd had too many daiquiris at the time, but——' She stared into Lola's rainy green eyes. 'You're in love with him, I take it?'

'I——' Lola's cheeks were touched with colour. 'I don't know. I don't think so, that is——'

'I may be past my best, sweetie, but I'm not blind yet,' Mrs Prenderghast said with a touch of her old sharpness. She eyed Lola. 'There's no time for talk now, more's the pity—but after all this is over, I shall want a complete explanation from both of you. Yes?'

'I promise, Mrs Prenderghast.'

'Then get dressed, quickly.'

Lola ran to her bedroom, and pulled clothes on hastily, her mind whirling. What had César meant by 'dynamite'? She'd just sent a lot of her clothes to the hotel laundry, and rather faded jeans and an embroidered cotton top were all she could find to wear. She stuffed a few toiletries into her bag, anticipating a longish stay away from the hotel. Would this mean she was now on the run from the police? She gnawed her full lower lip anxiously as she brushed her hair into some semblance of order. *Je t'aime.* . . . The words echoed through her mind. A meaningless phrase, meant to reassure her? A real statement of deep emotion? She might never know the answer.

Mrs Prenderghast was peering cautiously down the corridor as Lola emerged from her bedroom.

'They're still in Akhtopol's suite,' she hissed. Hurriedly, she pressed a huge pair of dark glasses on to Lola. 'Put these on—no one will recognise you.' Lola rather doubted that, but the garish things at least covered her face, and she put them on. Mamie nodded approval, then, unexpectedly, scrabbled in her purse, and pressed a fistful of banknotes into Lola's hand. 'Here—you may need money. Keep in touch, sweetie.' Lola hugged her swiftly, feeling close to tears.

'What are you g-going to tell them?' she whispered. 'They'll be furious with you for letting me go!'

'I shall tell them,' Mrs Prenderghast said with dignity, 'that I helped you escape. As for that monster, he doesn't frighten me. Get in touch with me when you can, sweetie. I'll be here, finishing *Unquenchable Flame of the Heart*. Yes?'

'Yes,' Lola promised. 'Bless you, too.' And then Mrs Prenderghast pushed her firmly out into the corridor. 'Run,' she whispered.

Lola ran.

As she passed the open door of Akhtopol's suite, she caught a glimpse of his burly figure stooping over the briefcase she'd opened last night. The little manager was solemnly looking under the bed. She scuttled past, her heart in her mouth, but no shout of anger showed that she'd been seen. She didn't dare risk alarming them with the telltale bell of the lift, so she ran down three flights of stairs before summoning it, and pressed the ground-floor button.

The journey down to the foyer was even worse than the one after stealing the tape last night.

What a hardened criminal she was becoming, all in the name of love ... But no hand descended on her shoulder, no burly figure blocked her way, and her heart soared at the sight of César, casually dressed and already waiting for her at a table near the door of the tea-room. He gave her a brief, almost harsh kiss, and minutes later they were in the car, on the way to St Jean.

Reaction made her want to just lean against him as he drove, her head on his shoulder. He rubbed his cheek against her temple, and she could feel the scrape of his beard against her skin.

'Did Akhtopol frighten you?' he asked gruffly. She nodded without replying. 'I should never have involved you in all this,' he muttered. 'Though God knows you seem to have pulled me out of the fire somehow!'

She straightened up. 'Really? So what *is* on that tape?'

'Financial deals, as we saw last night. But with a difference. I put it back on the computer early this morning,' he told her as they pulled up outside the villa, 'and checked it through. I don't know why, but I had a hunch there was something we'd missed.' He grinned at her, dazzlingly handsome. 'It took a while to find it, but the evidence is definitely there.'

'What evidence?' she demanded eagerly. They got out, and walked through the garden to the house.

'Evidence of Akhtopol's misdemeanours.' He took her arm. 'Our little Bulgarian friend has been stealing from his own company, as well as from me. He's been siphoning funds away from Cirrus for years. Not even in particularly clever way, I might add. It's a kind of computer-crime that's

very common these days. He simply adds a percent
or two to the various deals he makes, calls it
"commission"—meaning an official bribe to some
high-up official to secure the contract—and then
uses the computer to divert the money into his
own account in Switzerland.' César's tanned face
broke into a hard smile. 'One or two percent of the
kind of money Akhtopol deals with comes to large
figures, Lola. A nice rake-off, straight off the top,
and by my estimation, amounting to something
like a quarter of a million dollars a year.'

'God! So what are we going to do?' Lola asked.
'Go to the police?'

'I'm tempted,' César admitted as they entered
the long, bronze-tinted room. In today's brilliant
sunshine, the mood of the villa was one of
shimmering summer gold. 'It would serve
Akhtopol right. But there's a chance here for me
to get my tape back.'

'By blackmailing Akhtopol?'

'Let's say by bringing certain pressures to bear,'
César smiled. 'If Akhtopol still has that tape safe,
it's my guess he'll willingly swap it for his own one
back.' He picked up a jug of cold fruit-juice from
the snowy kitchen, tucked a digital telephone
under the other arm, and they walked through on
to the patio overlooking the dark blue sea. 'Cirrus
play rough,' he went on, opening the sun-umbrella
over the wrought-iron table. 'They have a
reputation for being very unforgiving towards
employees who try to rip them off. The temptation
to steal is always strong, and for salesmen like
Akhtopol the opportunities are always there, so
Cirrus keep a hard line.'

Lola relaxed in the chair, warm and happy, and
studied César. She never ceased to be amazed at

his physical presence, the sheer vitality that
crackled in his poise—even when, as now, he was
reclining by the sea in faded dungarees and a
cotton shirt, with all the lazy grace of a basking
leopard.

'But blackmail,' she said, studying the golden
eyes. 'That isn't exactly clean play, is it?'

'It isn't,' he grimaced. 'I don't like doing this,
Lola. It's not my style. But what choice do we
have? The tape that Poincarré stole is vital to
Aeromed, as you know.' He poured two dewy
glasses of juice, and stared out at the sea. 'I'd be
betraying all the people who work for me if I
didn't do everything in my power to get it back.
Besides which,' he added, wicked clefts appearing
at the corners of his smile, 'I have to admit that
I'm going to rather enjoy making Monsieur
Akhtopol sweat a little.' It was hard to resist his
smile, despite her nagging inner fear that what
César was proposing was a dangerous course.

'Are you sure?' she probed. 'Akhtopol looks as
though he could be quite nasty in a corner, César.'

'Trust me.' He leaned over to her, tilting her
chin up with his hand. His mouth was warm
against hers, his kiss bringing back bone-melting
memories of the night before. 'I have to take this
chance, little one. Akhtopol won't want to risk a
face-to-face encounter with me. As for his
defrauding Cirrus, that's between him and them. It
may be immoral, but frankly I don't give a damn
about it.' He stroked her cheek, staring at her face
with hooded eyes. 'Such soft green eyes,' he
murmured. 'And such an inviting mouth. Last
night meant a lot to me, Lola. And to you?'

'A lot,' she confirmed, dropping her eyes in
confusion.

'That is the way it should be.' He kissed her again, gently, and smiled into her eyes. 'Now— let's call Mr Akhtopol, and get him over with. Then we can spend the rest of the day on the beach. Okay?'

'Okay,' she agreed. As she watched him pick up the telephone and punch out the number, a wave of unreality crossed her mind. Could all this really be happening? Had she really just been kissed by the most fabulous man she'd ever met in her life, really seen the desire for her flare in his eyes? The glamour and danger of this moment were a thousand miles from her own sedate existence in England, with its drab present and boring future. It was as though a rainy London Sunday afternoon had suddenly been torn open to let in all the brilliance of a Mediterranean summer. Lola closed her long-lashed eyes against the sun. The intense blue sky above, the intensity of her own feelings for César Levertov, the intense incidents of the past weeks, all seemed to melt into a dream for a moment.

It's too beautiful to be true, she found herself thinking. This can't last—something's got to happen to take it all away from me, I know it. César was talking in slow, measured French now, and he glanced at her, as though he'd picked up her sudden vibration of anxiety and foreboding. The dark, utterly male face softened into a smile of reassurance for a second, and then he turned back to the receiver.

No, she whispered to herself. I'm not going to let you go, César. You mean too much to me. I've dreamed of you, burgled for you, been aroused to ecstasy by you—and you're mine! I'll fight for you if I have to, but I won't let you go!

Then, almost with surprise, she remembered that exciting and momentous events were taking place outside the world of her and César's emotions. She leaned forward, shaking the sense of unreality away, and tried to follow César's French. His face was expressionless, and she could faintly hear, above the whisper of the sea, the pygmy twitter of Akhtopol's voice. Patchily, she worked out that César was arranging a meeting-place of some kind. A stab of excitement went through her. So—it was working out! Had her bungled burglary actually done some good, after all? When at last he replaced the receiver, she was agog.

'Well?' she demanded breathlessly.

'Mr Akhtopol is a frightened man,' he said thoughtfully.

'Will he give you your tape back?'

'Yes.' A delighted grin spread across Lola's face, and he smiled at her in return, rather ruefully. 'It seems you're a better burglar than I am, little one.' His face grew thoughtful again. 'Whatever that tape contains, Akhtopol's desperate to get it back. He swears he hasn't communicated the Churchill plans yet—he didn't trust any of the commercial computer communications systems, and he says the Aeromed tape is still safe somewhere.'

'Oh, César!' Impulsively, she threw her arms around his neck, and hugged him. He held her close, stroking her hair.

'You succeeded after all, Lola. Why you risked your life on that balcony I'll never know—but it looks very much as though you've saved the Churchill for me.' He kissed her tenderly, and she looked up at him, bright-eyed with excitement.

'Is he going to bring the tape here?' she asked.

César shook his head.

'No. I don't trust him. He's going to leave the Aeromed tape at a specified place somewhere in Nice today—a letterbox attached to one of my construction sites—and we'll pick it up at our leisure. If we're satisfied, we'll post his tape back to him twenty-four hours later. He didn't like the arrangement, but he's scared enough to do anything. I also assured him that if he so much as spoke to you again, I'd ruin what little manhood he possesses.' He grinned fiercely. 'I wonder, though, why he's so very panic-stricken about getting the tape back. Maybe we've missed something . . .?'

'And the police?' she asked in some trepidation.

'He's in much too much trouble to go to the police,' César assured her. 'He was blustering in the hope of frightening you. He'd never have done it—so you're quite safe from the *gendarmerie*. He also knows I'd kill him if he touched you. Still, I want you to keep out of Akhtopol's way for the time being.'

'I will,' she grimaced, 'don't worry. But,' she went on, a thought suddenly striking her, 'what if he's made a copy of the plans?'

'We're going to keep a copy of his tape,' César replied calmly. 'He knows that, and he won't dare double-cross us. He has no option but to do exactly as we say.'

'So you've won,' she said wonderingly.

'*We've* won,' he corrected her softly. 'There would be nothing without you. This has been your show, my dear, from start to finish. I must find some way of thanking you, Lola.' She looked into the amber warmth of his eyes, the black pupils wide and compelling, and felt her heart contract.

The deadly seriousness of his expression softened into a smile. 'What about poor Mrs Prenderghast, though? She'll be dying of curiosity.'

'I'll phone her now,' Lola decided, 'and tell her everything's all right.' His hand rested on hers as she reached for the phone.

'Shall we take her out to dinner tonight—you and I?'

'That would be lovely,' Lola said warmly.

'Good. I know just the place. Oh—and ask her for the rest of the day off.' He raised his eyebrow at her expression. 'An afternoon in the sun is just what you need, Lola. Ask her.'

Mrs Prenderghast, delighted to hear that all was well, though bursting for enlightenment, did not demur when Lola asked. Her only concern seemed to be that Lola herself was safe and well, and she was touchingly excited at the prospect of going out with her and César that evening. It occurred to Lola for the first time that Mrs Prenderghast had scarcely been out for a single evening of this holiday—and that the writer's existence might be a cruelly lonely one at times.

'This is the most exciting thing that's happened to me in years,' Mrs Prenderghast was giggling as she rang off.

It was also rather humbling, Lola realised, to discover how much she'd misjudged Mamie Prenderghast. The old lady's spoiled ways had blinded her to the fact that underneath the crusty surface lurked a heart of gold—and from patent dislike, her own feelings for Mamie were steadily becoming ones of admiration and affection. How many other people, she wondered, had she misjudged in the same callow way? After she'd replaced the receiver, César took her hand, and stood up.

'*Bien*—and now let's forget all about Mr Akhtopol and the aeroplane for a few hours, and go down to the beach. We have many things to say to each other.'

CHAPTER SIX

THE water looked so delicious that Lola overcame her stab of jealousy at César's offer of a plain black one-piece costume, mysteriously found in a drawer somewhere in the villa. Midsummer was calling, and she firmly bit back her speculations about the costume's last wearer, and ran down with him to the private beach beside the villa, clutching his strong hand like a child.

The shimmering white beach was deserted, the solemn, stone-faced fishermen's cottages smiling down at them from the palm-lined esplanade. Suddenly feeling twelve years old again, she ran to the water's cool edge, and plunged in. He followed, his tanned body slicing efficiently through the water after her. It was bakingly hot as the sun neared midday, and the mood was one of joyous celebration. She turned to face him as he swam up to her, and he took her in his arms. His body was smooth and hard against hers, the warmth of his flesh touching her through the cool water.

'My little burglar,' he smiled, his golden eyes tender. Her own body was shy, her skin flinching from the intimacy of the near-naked embrace. A small wave washed over them, tugging them gently apart for a moment—and then they were locked together again, dripping mouths meeting. The kiss was salt at first, then sweet. She clung to the smooth power of his shoulders, lost in the domination he seemed able to exert over her so easily—a domination she'd never been able to accept from any other man, yet which now seemed to exalt her very soul with delight. If this was not love, then it was something very close. He had the ability to lose her, to float her into another world, where only she and he mattered. Her trust for him was an incredible thing—an emotion that was already fully formed and mature. She would have trusted him with her life, her soul, as easily as she trusted her slender body to his strong arms in this cool sea.

She caressed his wet hair with inexpert, tender fingers, and felt him draw her body close against his. Again, the sea nudged at them, the breakers creaming around their shoulders, and he drew back, grinning at her sexily.

'We're meant to be cooling off—not overheating!'

'César,' she asked impulsively, before she could stop herself, 'how much do I mean to you?'

'How much?' he repeated. The strikingly handsome face was whimsical.

'You say there's something special between us,' she pressed, treading water and staring into his beautiful eyes. 'But what am I to you? A casual affair?' Feeling her face redden, she stumbled on, 'B—because you mean a lot to me, César. Nothing——' She groped for the words, her green eyes intent. 'Nothing like this has ever happened to me before, and I don't want to be hurt.' She bit her lip to stop any more clumsy words from tumbling out—next she'd be asking him the unaskable—whether he loved her, whether he was going to betray her.

César's expression was suddenly compassionate. 'I know what you risked for me, Lola. And that gives me a pretty good idea what I mean to you. I care a lot for you, too. I mean that. But if you want me to tell you I'm head over heels in love with you——' He shook his head with a wry smile. 'I can't do that, no matter how much I might want to. It would be false. Deep emotions take time to develop—and more than that, it takes time to test them.' Lola nodded, though she was reflecting with a touch of sadness that it hadn't taken very long for *her* emotions to reach a depth she could never have believed. Yet what he said rang true, and as he touched her cheek, his hand was gentle.

'I'll say this,' he said quietly. 'I think my feelings for you are going to become very serious. Much more serious than anything I've ever felt for a woman before. I understand your fear that all this may end tomorrow but——' He shrugged, bronzed lips curving into a bittersweet smile. '—that's also possible. I don't want to deceive you.' He kissed her firmly. 'I just ask you to have patience. And have faith! Let's stretch our muscles a little, sweet one. Okay?'

'Okay,' she nodded, trying to answer his smile. She followed his lazy, efficient crawl through the water, feeling a mixture of emotions. At least he'd been honest, almost brutally so. And at least he'd left her with the hope that what was growing between them might, on his side, become the love she so badly needed. The alternative was not something she cared to contemplate. César Levertov had entered her life, and shaken it upside down. If his feelings for her came to nothing, she knew that for her it would be the most destructive event since her mother's death.

More serious than anything I've ever felt for a woman before. How many women? And what had he felt for them? The question, motivated as much by curiosity as by jealousy, stayed in her mind—and when, half-an-hour later, they stretched out panting on the baking sand, she cupped her chin in her palms, and stared thoughtfully at his face, wondering.

He towelled his dark hair dry, and met her eyes. 'How old are you, Lola?'

'Twenty-two,' she answered, and flushed a little at the wry arch of his eyebrows. 'And you?'

'Old enough to be—well, not exactly your father, but a much older brother. The right side of forty, anyway. Does that put you off?'

'Why should it?' She glanced at the sleek, panther-like lines of his golden torso, then dropped her eyes. 'Women are supposed to go for older men—and besides, you aren't exactly ancient.'

'That's nice to know,' he grinned, showing excellent white teeth. In truth, there was a kind of majesty to his body. The tight muscles and the lithe planes of stomach and hips spoke of an active life, and there were huge reserves of power in the long legs and the deep chest. There was a hard maturity to César's body that she found irresistibly exciting, even a little frightening—an ultra-masculine aura that whipped at her senses. She'd never found the male anatomy attractive before. She was finding César's stunning.

'Your mother died a few years ago,' he said directly. She nodded. 'How?' She told him about the disaster with the intravenous drip, and he listened quietly. Assessing her own emotions as she described her own desolation after the tragedy, Lola was struck by the ease with which she was able to communicate with him. There was a depth of understanding in him which she hadn't found in men her own age—a sense that he understood. Understood not only what her clumsy words could say, but the unspoken things, the experiences too deep for words, that only the most compassionate and thoughtful mind could reach after.

'I still get great waves of self-pity,' she concluded with a slight smile. 'It's very easy to feel that you owe the world a grudge when something like that has happened.'

'Easy—and natural,' he commented. 'How did your father take it?'

'That's very hard to say,' she confessed, thinking of the silver-haired, cool-eyed man who was her father. Even before her mother's death, he'd been a reserved, self-contained person. 'He's a man who doesn't find it easy to express his emotions. It's almost as though all the years he's spent in business have schooled him to keep all feeling locked away inside, to show nothing.'

'Unlike you,' César suggested with a smile.

'I get my thin skin from my mother,' she acknowledged. 'I know that Dad suffered a great deal when Mum died, but he's hardly ever spoken to either me or Tom about it. And we've both been too shy of him to ask.'

'Perhaps that's a pity,' César said thoughtfully. 'Those who seem the strongest among us are sometimes the ones who most need comfort. Maybe you should learn to understand him better.'

Lola nodded, appreciating the truth in Cesar's words. 'In a way,' she confessed, idly drawing patterns in the warm sand, 'I still feel that I don't completely know him. I love him—Tom and I both do, and we respect him deeply. But as for the person he is inside——' She shook her head. Who on earth *did* know the person who lay behind that serious, quiet façade? She'd been shy of her father ever since she could remember.

Now was perhaps the time to face that shyness, and begin to understand what he was really like. Maybe, with Ceśar at her side, she could enter a completely new phase of her relationship with her father?

Hold it right there, she cautioned herself fiercely. Don't start making future plans that include César, unless you want your heart broken!

'You told me your parents had died while you were in your teens,' she said, shifting the subject. He nodded confirmation. 'Tell me about them,' she invited.

He rolled on to his back, and pulled her close to him, so that she was lying across his body, and studied the petal-soft pinkness of her full mouth with speculative eyes. The touch of their naked skins was like a transfusion of hot wine into her blood, and she had to fight down the surge of passion in her heart. 'And what exactly do you want to know?' he purred, managing to look exactly like a very beautiful, very hungry panther.

'About you.' Timidly, her slim fingers stroked their way through the crisp dark hair of his chest, and she veiled her eyes from the directness of his gaze with conveniently thick lashes. 'About how you grew up, what made you the way you are. Was your grandfather really a Russian Count?'

'Of course,' he smiled. 'His name was Alexei Alexeivitch Levertov, and he was third cousin to the Tsarina. A handsome young fool. He escaped by the skin of his teeth in 1917, and came to France like so many of the Russian *émigrés*.'

'And met your grandmother?'

'Yes. Barbara Gabriel, Countess of Calvados-Eure. He rescued her from a wild boar during a hunt. It was evidently love at first sight.'

'Indeed,' Lola murmured, fielding his wicked grin. Close up, she was marvelling at the fineness of his skin; for all the iron-hardness of his muscles, it was like deep golden velvet. 'Do I detect a note of cynicism about your noble ancestors, Monsieur Levertov?'

'Cynicism?' His face softened. 'No, Lola. I loved my parents—and my grandparents too, what I remember of them. They all died young, partly because they all lived too fast for their own good. But there are things about them that I find it hard to accept.' He stroked her salty blonde hair affectionately. 'For one thing, Alexei Alexeivitch was a hopeless romantic just like you. All his life he believed that the Bolshevik revolution was just a passing phase, and that Communism was going to collapse at any minute—so that he, and the other aristocrats, would be begged to return and rule over all the Russias, just as they'd done before. Worse still, he filled my father's mind with this idea from his earliest days. Grandfather wouldn't permit my father to learn a thing beyond riding and shooting, wouldn't let him think of working for his living. That wasn't *aristocratic*.' César's face was ironic. 'On the other hand, Grandfather had brought only a few jewels and icons with him when he fled—and the Calvados-Eure family were busy selling off the last few thousand acres of their estates by the time he and my grandmother met, so when the promised victory failed to materialise, my parents suddenly discovered that the spring they'd been living on had suddenly dried up. They were penniless, and quite without the means of earning anything more.'

'What were they like?' Lola asked, fascinated.

'I remember my grandfather as a dapper, rather secretive old man. He was always going off to some mysterious meeting or other with various shady ex-Imperial Army cronies of his. He lived in a kind of fantasy world, full of plots and conspiracies against the Soviet state. All nonsense, of course—just a sad bunch of old men trying to make their dreams last a little longer. My parents were beautiful creatures, especially my mother. She had the most remarkable violet eyes, and hair just a shade lighter than yours. Utterly impractical, both of them.' He touched Lola's satiny cheek ruefully. 'For them, life was all hunting and dances and expensive cars—a life lived on credit and expectations. The harsh years after the Second World War spelled the end of the dream, though. By the time I was born, a few years after the end of the war, harsh reality was catching up with them. However, I don't think they ever fully realised it, which was just as well; they died with all their dreams still more or less intact. I was sixteen when they were both killed in a car-crash. Grandfather Levertov didn't survive them by much; he was only in his late sixties. but the shock of their death killed him.' He kissed her softly, as though touched by her bereaved expression. 'A catalogue of tragedy, *n'est-ce-pas*? At sixteen, though, one is luckily too young to have much appreciation of tragedy. I discovered that he who does not work does not eat—unless he is prepared to accept the humiliating charity that the state metes out to orphans and paupers.'

'What did you do?' she prompted, trying to imagine this powerful, self-assured man as a hungry boy, and finding it very difficult.

'I managed to get work in an engineering firm in Paris. I already knew what I wanted to do—to build my own airplanes, and fly them through the sky. I worked in the factory for three years to finance my way through college. Then, when I was twenty-one, I had a stroke of great good luck. I won a scholarship to study aerodynamics at Caltech, in America. From then on, things began to get a lot easier.' He sat up, smiling. 'And that's enough about me for the time being. Tell me about Lola now.'

'You already know all about me,' she protested. 'And you were just getting to the intriguing part!'

'You mean my youthful indiscretions?' he queried with a grin. 'I shall have to know a little about yours, first.'

'I don't think I had any,' she confessed ruefully.

'Really?' His smile was pure sin. 'Perhaps we ought to start remedying that right now!'

The manager came bustling out to meet Lola when César dropped her off at the hotel in the late afternoon. He was all apologies, his face beaming with relief and pleasure. Monsieur Akhtopol, it turned out, had been mistaken, and had abjectly withdrawn all charges against her only a few hours ago. The man had been quite shaken, the manager assured her, and was most conciliatory.

'I was in any case convinced, Mademoiselle,' he said confidentially, 'that you had had nothing to do with his tape. Frankly, guests like Monsieur Akhtopol bring down the tone of any hotel.'

Lola nodded guiltily, and went up to the suite, wondering whether everything could really have worked out so perfectly. Mrs Prenderghast, agog with excitement and curiosity, bustled Lola into a hot bath to wash off the salt and sand before going out again. After Lola had emerged, though, Mrs Prenderghast came into her bedroom to find her sitting absently on the bed, still wrapped in her towel. The hot bath had been relaxing—but had also left her deep in thought.

'Aren't you dressed yet? You'd better hurry,' she warned. 'César is coming to pick us up in forty minutes, you know.' Lola glanced at the evening sky, which was already darkening, and nodded.

'Sorry. I was in a reverie.'

'I'm not surprised—a lot has happened to you,' Mamie said enviously. She paused for a moment, then held something out to Lola. 'I thought you might like these, sweetie. You don't have any, do you?'

Lola stared at the slim string of pearls, and blinked up at her employer in surprise.

'They're not very big,' Mrs Prenderghast said self-consciously. 'But they're very good quality. I bought them in Japan last year, but I've never worn them. Go on—take them.'

'But Mrs Prenderghast——' Genuinely moved, Lola held the softly gleaming things up to the light. 'They're beautiful! I couldn't possibly——'

'Of course you could,' Mrs Prenderghast said, almost gruffly. 'They'll look better on you than they ever did on me. Besides, when a girl's being taken out by her beau, she wants a little something to make her feel more confident.' A touch of her old asperity crept back, as though she'd been embarrassed by her own gesture of affection. 'Now don't dawdle, Lola,' she commanded, and bustled out.

Touched to her heart, Lola could only stare after the retreating back and wonder. The pearls were indeed beautiful, matched to perfection, and had probably cost a great deal. She pressed the cool strand to her lips, and closed her eyes. Yes, she'd misjudged Mamie. The expression on her employer's face as César had brought her back had shown her how much Mamie Prenderghast had really been worried about her. A quick sense of shame for all the harsh thoughts she'd had about Mamie brought the colour to her cheeks, and she fastened the pearls around her neck, making up her mind never to let another unfair criticism pass her lips.

And Mamie had been right—a lot *had* happened to her. There'd been so little time to think on the rollercoaster of the past few days, dangerously little time. Things were happening very fast. How long was she going to be able to keep up with them—and with César? As she sat on the bed to easy her only pair of good stockings over her slim calves, Lola thought back to the fiery glow of that night at César's villa. To many women, she knew, the excitement and passion she'd experienced that night would be a common occurrence, something to be accepted as natural. To her it was unforgettable, the dream of a lifetime become reality.

César had arrived like some Arthurian knight at the gates of her little castle, and sent all the stones crashing to the ground, leaving her free, but also fatally vulnerable. Could a man like César Levertov really have any interest in her beyond the quick excitement of a sexual conquest? He was kind, and said things that made her heart tremble—but didn't all men say those things to get their own way?

That moment of unreality this morning had deepened into a nagging depression. Why? She'd never been as insecure as this before. Hating herself for the thought, she couldn't help remembering that César would have his stolen tape back very soon. And though she couldn't believe that César had used her as a means to an end—he wasn't that callous—the tape had been the direct cause of their first meeting. When he had it back, might his interest in her not abruptly fade away? They had so very little in common except the shared thrill of an adventure, an adventure that was rapidly drawing to an end. That was her worst fear, and it hurt to admit it.

She opened the cupboard, trying to forget her worries for the time being, and took out the simple gown in pale gold that was almost the only formal dress she'd brought with her. She'd bought it just before leaving London, with the expectation of wearing it for the odd concert or evening occasion, and it had been a strangely out-of-character choice for her, with its bare back and low neckline. She slipped it on, sliding the straps over the tanned skin of her shoulders. The vee of the neckline plunged low between her breasts, even lower than she'd remembered. The contrast between the fine material and her silky skin was startlingly sensual. The past weeks in the Mediterranean sun had burned her skin darker, and brought out the usual sprinkling of freckles, flecks of bronze against wild honey. For once, though, she didn't mind them; they were a reminder of her youth and freshness.

More worrying was the fact of having to go

braless; the full swell of her breasts was provocative against the shimmering material, and she knew she was going to be looked at tonight. That wasn't something she necessarily enjoyed. Her residual shyness was still there, deep inside. But the almost wicked sexiness would probably appeal to César!

She studied herself in the mirror with a strange expression on her face. She'd never worn clothes like this before, had never set out to package her body in a way that male eyes would find desirable. Was she changing so very quickly?

She scooped the heavy golden hair away from the slender column of her neck, and went to sit at the dressing-table. *Be careful*, she warned her face in the mirror silently. Don't give away too much tonight!

Her make-up bag waited on the table. Tonight, if ever, was an occasion for a grand cosmetic production, but suddenly she felt she didn't want to plaster her face with make-up. It would be too easy to hide behind paint and feel that false sense of security that cosmetics would bring. She settled on doing her eyes and mouth, leaving the gilded satin of her face clean. Maybe that would make her look absurdly young, but she didn't mind that. Honesty was her only defence right now.

Soft grey-green eye-shadow complemented her eyes, and her long lashes needed only a touch of mascara to bring out their full dramatic potential. She spent more time, though, over her mouth, covering the velvet of her lips with gloss, and delineating the soft curves with a fine brush to emphasise their grace. As she entered her early twenties, she was beginning to have more and more of her mother's look about her.

Zara Golightly had been born Zara Rossini, the daughter of an Italian doctor and an English nurse, and she had had the golden skin and raven hair of her father's side of the family. That Mediterranean inheritance was beginning to appear in Lola's own face now in the beautiful bone-structure and the wide, long-lashed eyes that she remembered so well from her mother. In her late teens Lola had been pretty. Now, she realised without vanity, she was growing into real beauty. Maybe it was the southern sun over the past weeks, or perhaps it was even the tiredness that still lurked under her eyes and at the corners of her mouth, but tonight she knew she was ravishing. No longer a girl, but a woman in the full bloom of her femininity. And perhaps that, too, was something to do with her maturing emotion for César. Perhaps it took love to unfold those last few petals of beauty, and bring the flower to fullness.

And perhaps it would take love to make it fade, as unexpectedly and rapidly.

'What an *extraordinary* story,' Mamie Prender-ghast said, leaning back with the contented expression of someone who'd been royally enter-tained. The soft lights of the club flattered her painted face, making her look five years younger, and Lola and César glanced at each other with a smile. They'd been explaining the Akhtopol story—or as much of it as wasn't private between them—to her, and she'd been listening spellbound. 'I'm a professional storyteller,' she said, sipping at her fifth daiquiri of the evening, 'but you've held me absolutely enthralled. What I can't understand, though,' she said plaintively, looking at Lola, 'is why you didn't let me in on the secret *ages* ago?'

'Lola didn't want to worry you,' César replied diplomatically.

'It would take more than that monster to worry *me*. I always knew he was up to no good! I'm going to turn this into a novel,' she promised. 'It has all the requirements—a monster, a beautiful damsel——' she ogled César extravagantly'—and a *dreamy* hero.'

César grinned. He was, Lola thought quietly, indeed magnificent. Somehow formal wear suited him best, bringing out the aristocratic lineage that tamed the raw energy of his nature. Satin and silk matched the velvety quality that was his most dangerous asset, sheathing as it did the steel of his claws.

It was turning out an extremely successful evening. The meal at the restaurant, the first roast pheasant of the season, had been superb, satisfying even Mamie's pampered tastes. It had also been a reminder of the fulness of the year, and the imminence of autumn. The hint of melancholy that had crept into Lola's soul late in the afternoon was still there, and she knew she hadn't been exactly sparkling company this evening. She couldn't rid herself of the fear that whatever it was she had with César might be drawing to a close, already, before it had even started.

César had been at his most charming, treating Mamie with understanding and kindness. In his company, Mamie's angular personality softened, becoming gentle, almost sweet. The isolation of wealth, self-indulgence and loneliness, Lola reflected, had been the chief causes of Mamie Prenderghast's unlikeability—and César seemed to understand that, seemed to be able to bring out the reservoir of genuineness in the woman. He'd managed to make her gurgle with laughter the whole evening long. Everything had seemed amusing, even the squeeze of getting all three of them into the Lamborghini, and the light sprinkle of rain that had caught them unawares outside the night-club.

He leaned forward to study the pearls, his warm fingers brushing the delicate skin of her shoulder as he lifted the strand to the light.

'You have excellent taste, Mamie,' he purred. 'These couldn't have been better chosen to suit Lola. Pearls are the gems of virginity and purity.' His eyes teased her as he spoke, smoky, thrilling eyes that brought the blood swiftly to her throat and cheeks. In the same gentle tone, almost inaudible to Mamie, he murmured, 'Have I told you yet how ravishingly lovely you are tonight?'

'Thank you,' she said awkwardly, tearing her eyes away from his with an effort. She'd felt his eyes on her all night, warm and desiring, and each time she'd looked up to meet that dark gaze it was as though an invisible spark of secret electricity leaped between them.

Mamie was looking at them roguishly. There was little doubt that she imagined them to be in the midst of a full-blown affair, and somehow that upset Lola. 'This place is very nice,' she commented rather woodenly.

'It's more than that,' Mamie decided firmly, glancing round the elegant, beautifully lit room. 'It's beautiful.' The five-piece band were playing smooth dancing jazz, and the atmosphere was exciting, distinctly French. At the next table, two good-looking young men escorting identical pout-ing brunettes kept glancing at her, obviously discussing her with interest—to the chagrin of the brunettes. At the restaurant, too, she'd felt male attention hover round her. A new experience for Lola Golightly, she realised wryly. Although she'd been drinking only sips of dry champagne, Lola's head was beginning to feel light.

César took her hand under the tablecloth, his eyes probing hers. 'Is anything wrong, *chérie*?' he asked softly.

'I'm just tired,' she told him, looking down.

'I'm thoughtless. Of course you must be exhausted. We won't stay long,' he promised. 'One dance in a few minutes, then I'll take you home.'

'Home?' Mamie looked up from her drink. 'Did I hear someone say something about going home?'

'I was just saying that Lola looks tired,' César said his eyes still holding Lola's.

'Nonsense,' Mamie chuckled. 'She's having the time of her life—aren't you, sweetie?' Lola smiled rather feebly, and Mamie gulped down the rest of her daiquiri and glanced slightly tipsily at her watch. 'As for me, old crock that I am—you can take me home soon, César. But you two go on and enjoy yourselves for the rest of the evening. The night is yet young!'

'I really——' Lola began, but Mamie waved an imperious hand.

'And I don't want to see you back before dawn,' she commanded. 'Summer nights are for lovers!'

Lola winced at the word. *Lovers* . . . She felt César's thumb caress the back of her hand, and her fingers trembled inside his. Her yearning for him was so strong, so deep . . . Did he know that by merely holding her hand he could make her feel as nervous as a schoolgirl on her first date? She sat quiet, listening to him entertaining Mamie. He was so poised, so at ease. It was typical of him to know the most elegant places in Nice, yet to treat the whole evening with a charming casualness. He was never pompous, never solemn.

'How's *Unquenchable Flame of the Heart* going?' César was asking.

'I'm on the last few pages,' Mamie told them happily. 'Armand has come to a gory end under the 5:55 from Brighton to London, and Laetitia is reconciling herself to marrying Terry at last. The formula never fails.'

'I'm glad it doesn't apply to real life,' César commented. 'In our case, Lola would end up with Mr Akhtopol, and I'd be conveniently run over on the esplanade.'

Mamie chuckled. 'I haven't seen Akhtopol since he came bursting into our suite. Gone into hiding, I shouldn't wonder.' She cocked an eye at César. 'So you see yourself as a romantic hero? Does that mean you're planning to carry Lola off and marry her, César?'

Lola could have kicked her employer under the table, but César was unperturbed.

'That would be the romantic thing to do, *n'est-ce-pas*?' His eyes dropped to caress Lola's mouth. 'There would be compensations, ah yes. Yet they say that marriage is an un-economic proposition for a man.'

'Un-economic?' Mamie enquired.

'"Any man",' he quoted gently, '"who is willing to sacrifice his interests to get possession of a pretty face is a fool. Pretty faces are to be had cheaper than that." And before you jump down my throat,' he smiled, 'a woman said that.'

'A woman said that,' Lola agreed sharply, 'in a book written by a man.' Her eyes glinted like angry emeralds. The quotation had disturbed her; hearing the words on his lips had stirred her deepest anxieties about César.

'*Touché,*' he nodded. 'Yet you'll agree that there's a great deal of human truth in *The Warden*?'

'Yes,' Lola shrugged, dropping dark lashes over her eyes again, 'but not necessarily on the lips of its most cynical characters.' The lights on the dance floor had dimmed to a soft red haze, and the band had eased into a slow, sinuous version of *Caravan*. César rose in one fluid motion, and tugged at Lola's hand. 'I stand rebuked, then. Would you excuse us, Mamie? I'd like to dance with my rescuer.'

Lola was feeling depressed and dizzy as she allowed him to lead her through the tables to the dance floor where a dozen couples were moving to the sensuous Latin tempo. And as they stepped on to the smooth surface, he took her in his arms with possessive strength. The blood raced to her temples as he drew her close in the hazy ruby glow, the hard length of his body warm against hers, and it was an effort to concentrate on the dancing.

'What's wrong tonight?' His breath was warm in her ear. 'Have I upset you?'

'No,' she denied. 'I told you, I'm just a bit run down.'

'And that's all?'

'That's all.'

'Little liar.' His kiss brushed against her eyelids. 'You don't trust me, do you?'

'Of course I do, César!' But she could hear the insincerity in her own voice as she spoke.

'Of course you do,' he repeated drily, and changed the subject. 'Mamie seems to be having a good time. She has a great capacity for enjoying herself.'

'You've been very kind to her,' Lola replied, and looked up at him, her thick blonde hair falling in a tumble of gold down her naked back. 'You bring out the best in her. I think she's secretly extremely lonely.'

'The old are always lonely,' he said, touching her cheek. 'They deserve more love than they get from the young.'

They had edged towards the darkness at the back of the dance floor, and he looked down at her with deep amber eyes. 'Your body is as stiff as a doll's. Don't you like dancing?'

'Sorry,' she gritted, consciously trying to relax. The music was sensual, dreamlike, and the sculpted presence of his body against hers was like a rock in a twilight sea. He drew her close, his thigh pressing between hers in time to the rhythm. His mouth caressed the soft skin of her cheek, reaching her ear with an intoxication of warm breath. Relaxation spread through her veins like warm honey, bringing with it the desire for him that possessed her like a sharp ache.

'You're so lovely tonight, Lola, like a young queen. I'm sorry, is that a cliché?' He smiled with dark eyes. 'You're magnificent in that dress. I can't take my eyes off you, your skin, your hair, your hands. You make me burn to possess you, my sweet, plumb the depth of that mystery . . .' His teeth tugged at her earlobe, making her gasp softly. 'But you're trembling like a leaf,' he murmured. 'Do I frighten you that much?'

'You know very well what you do to me,' she

whispered, aware that she was indeed shaking in his arms.

'Then don't flutter those cool green eyes at me,' he growled, his hands sliding down her slender body to settle hungrily on her hips. 'You couldn't make me want you any more than I do. Would you like to go anywhere else after this?'

'I don't think so,' she said hesitantly. 'Maybe just back to the Grande.' The red glow had turned his face into a handsome mask. She caught the glint of his smile.

'So soon! Tonight should be a celebration, no?'

'You haven't got your tape back yet,' she pointed out. And found herself almost wishing that he'd never get it back, so this idyll could go on for ever without ever reaching the harsh light of reality.

'Akhtopol will have already dropped it off by now,' he said. 'I'll go to the site and pick it up first thing tomorrow morning.'

'Can I come?' she pleaded, looking up into his dark face.

'What for?' he shrugged. 'That won't be necessary.'

'I see.' Lola bit her lip, and looked away. She was already being edged out! Her usefulness had come to an end, and her part in César's life was now over . . .

Deliberately, he tilted her chin up, and kissed her mouth. She couldn't respond to the warm pressure, and he smiled rather wryly down at her.

'Your lips are cold, little one. I think perhaps it is time I took you home, after all.'

'I'm perfectly all right,' she snapped, torn between her inability to dismiss her haunting fears and her ache to have this dance last for ever.

'You sound like an over-tired little girl,' he purred. 'A little girl who doesn't know what she wants.' This time, as his mouth found hers, she felt her lips opening to receive his kiss—that sweet invasion which she'd learned to yearn for.

César's effect on her was a force that seemed to grow with each encounter they had; it called to her, commanding her response more surely, more powerfully each time. Already, she knew, she was utterly his, emotionally as well as physically. She was being forced to acknowledge a need for him that was more powerful than any emotion she'd ever known.

'You had the same expression on your face the day I took you up in the jet,' he said, watching her misty eyes.

'I'm as dizzy now as I was then,' she said unevenly.

'Let's drop Mamie off and go for a walk along the beach,' he murmured against her ear as the number came to an end and the lights brightened. They'd barely been moving, utterly absorbed in one another, and as the band launched into a fast swing number, bringing several more couples on to the floor, she swayed giddily against him. 'Yes?'

'Yes,' she nodded, clinging to him.

'Come then.' He led her off the dance floor, his arm supporting her.

CHAPTER SEVEN

THE sand was still warm under their bare feet, and the soft rumble of the breakers was like a lullaby beside them. The moon was down, and the sea was only a glimmer in the darkness, but the lights of Nice were a cobweb of diamonds in the distance.

They'd dropped Mamie off at the hotel half an hour ago, then driven down to the sea, and parked the car at the edge of the beach. He'd pulled off his jacket and tie, and she could feel the heat of his body through his shirt as she walked with him over the yielding dunes, snuggling close against his side. The sea air was tangy, salt as tears.

'We won't be able to do this in Scotland,' he mused. 'British nights are not so kind—and the autumn will have set in by then.'

'Do you really mean that?' she asked before she could stop herself. 'I mean, about coming to England next month?'

'Of course I mean it,' he said, sounding puzzled. 'Why shouldn't I mean it?'

'No reason,' she said in a small voice. He stopped and pulled her round to face him. The breeze tugged her hair in a golden veil around her face, and she pushed it back to try and see his expression in the darkness.

'What is all this, Lola? You've been like death at the feast tonight. Are you afraid that I'm going to leave you?'

'I can't help it,' she said miserably. 'This means

so much to me, César. I'm so uncertain inside, so afraid.'

'For God's sake,' he said almost angrily. 'Can't you see how much I want you? Lola, I can't believe you don't feel what I feel when we touch or look at each other. You know how special this is. What makes you doubt me?'

'Well——' She hesitated unhappily. 'Like tonight—you said you didn't want me to come with you to pick up the tape.'

'Is *that* what this is all about?'

'Partly,' she confessed. 'Oh César I'm so sure that once you've got your tape back you'll lose interest in me——'

'Crazy little Lola!' He held her close. 'You really want to know why I said that? Because I want to pick it up before anyone else arrives at the site office—and you look as though you could do with a lie-in tomorrow.' He kissed her forehead. 'Also because I don't want to risk you bumping into Akhtopol if he should decide to be there. That's all!'

'Really?'

'Really!'

'But César,' she pointed out, her heart lifting joyfully, 'I've already experienced both of those discomforts for your sake, you know.'

His laugh was deep, amused.

'True enough—and I don't think there's anything I could do that would stop you coming. I must have been crazy to try. This is your triumph, Lola, not mine; and you shall be there. Am I forgiven?'

'Almost.' She held her face up for his lips, her mood suddenly absurdly happy. What small things it took to reassure her anxious heart!

He drew her down on to the warm sand, and they lay together in the hollow of a dune, Lola's head cradled on César's chest. The beach was totally deserted, and in the dunes even the lights of Nice were invisible in the night. Only the sparkle of two or three ships, far out to sea, indicated any human presence. 'Scotland is going to be wonderful,' he said dreamily. 'More than wonderful. We'll have oceans of time for each other, the stillness of nature to hear each others' heartbeats. Ah, Lola, how I love these moments alone with you. I know you think I'm obsessed with the Churchill—but I'm not. She's beginning to mean less and less to me, in fact. Nothing seems to satisfy me now.' He caressed the silky swathe of her hair roughly. 'Not the factory, not the villa, not even flying any more. The only things that do please me are the things I can share with you. Like tonight. Like now.' The murmur of the sea filled the silence for a while as she lay against his warm body, aching for him to go on. 'I want you, very badly. That much you must know by now. But this isn't just a physical thing, not any more. It seems to be growing inside me, spreading right through me like——' He shook his head, unable to find the right words. 'To tell you the truth, my sweet, it disturbs me. It's as much a pain as it is a pleasure. You make me so very restless, *ma petite*. I'm not sure whether that's a good thing or not.'

'*I* think it is,' she said breathlessly. 'If only I had the words to tell you how you make *me* feel, César!'

'You don't need words,' he whispered, drawing her close. 'The touch of your lips is enough . . .' Her body moved with languid urgency in his arms as their mouths touched; an urgency that was suddenly languid no longer, but shuddering and taut.

Her need to be loved by him was a hunger that she could never satisfy. Other times they'd kissed had been gentle, almost shy; now it was as though they couldn't have enough of each other. It was like an addiction, this need to be utterly one, touching in every inch of their bodies and souls. He crushed her to him, his teeth sharp on her throat, almost as though he would like to have bitten her there, marking her as his own for ever.

'César, I need you so much,' she heard herself say huskily. 'Don't ever leave me, ever!'

'Leave you?' His teeth punished her lower lip for the words. 'We're chained together, Lola. There's no leaving, no parting now. There never can be.' He propped himself up beside her, and she saw the glimmer of his smile in the darkness. 'Let's swim.'

'What, now?' she smiled.

'Yes, now,' he commanded. 'You are decent under that dress, aren't you?'

'Well,' she hesitated, thinking of the delicate, translucent material of her underwear, and her bra-less state. But it was, after all, night time. 'Sort of——'

'Come on, then!'

'My crazy love,' she said, gurgling with laughter.

'Clothes are just the manacles of civilisation, anyway,' he grinned. He was already undressing, and the idea was suddenly delicious to her. She tugged off the golden dress, grateful for the soft darkness that disguised the skimpiness of her lacy underwear. The warm night air was sweet on her skin, and she was still laughing as he took her hand, and they walked down to the glimmering line of the sea's edge. 'Is this your idea of a cold shower?' she teased him.

'Something like that,' he confessed. 'No turning back!' He tugged her hand as she tried to scamper away from the cool splash of the wavelets, and their near-naked bodies brushed briefly together as he hustled her into the water.

She squealed, spluttering salt; but the coolness was delightful against her hot skin, and she let him lead her out into the deeper water. His hands, so sure and strong, were linked through hers. He drew her close as they floated in the waves.

'Look at the stars.' They were brilliant tonight, even brighter for the absence of the moon, and she arched her neck to follow the gleaming track of the Milky Way.

'They're not nearly as bright as that in England,' she sighed. His lips met hers, wet and smiling, and he pulled her tight against him. She felt, rather than heard, his laugh. 'What's so funny?' she demanded.

'You are,' he murmured. 'You've changed so much. When first we met, you were quite the primmest little spinster I'd ever met. Kissing you was like kissing a marble statue. And now here you are, practically naked in my arms in the sea at midnight, your mouth as warm as mulled wine.'

'Then it's you who's responsible for my corruption,' she accused pointedly.

'Did I say I didn't like it?' His hand traced the sweet curves of her body. 'Sometimes I think you're a modern-day Circe,' he said, his eyes half-serious. 'You've bewitched me, Lola.'

'Then why is it always me who suffers?' she smiled wryly. 'You can do exactly as you please with me! You're so cool, César, always in command.'

'You think so?' He kissed her again, his mouth holding a hint of fierceness, and she could feel his muscles as tense as steel springs against her. Her thrill of pleasure at the force of his response to her was short-lived—he suddenly pushed her firmly away. 'Let's go back to the car.'

'But why?' she demanded, puzzled at his reaction, and aching to be in his arms again.

'Because I say so.'

'Well *I* say not,' she said petulantly, and curled up against him again, twining her arms round his neck and seeking his mouth with her lips.

'You don't know what you're doing to me, Lola,' he said roughly. 'We'd better get back into the manacles of civilisation within the next thirty seconds, or——'

'Or what?' she asked, trying to sound coy, but only sounding very shaky. He ignored her question scornfully, and instead of a kiss, his teeth nipped her lower lip sharply.

'I must be crazy,' he muttered. 'Cradle-snatching like this!' There was formidable strength in his arms as he scooped her up, and carried her back to the beach, her hands clasped around his neck.

'Damn it, César,' she spluttered, 'I don't understand you sometimes. I'm not a child any more! I know what I want!'

'And what *do* you want?' he asked, his dark face enigmatic.

'I want——' Her own voice sounded small in her ears. She stared up into his face mutinously. 'I want to stay in the water—with you!'

'*Ah, oui?*' He let her slide unceremoniously to

her feet, and scooped up her discarded dress.
'Here,' he said, presenting her with the bundle,
'take your chance before I change my mind!'

'I hate being laughed at,' she exploded,
snatching the dress out of his hands. 'You were the
one who wanted to swim—and just when it was
beautiful you decide to go back to the car! I'm not
some toy you can just wind up and then stop!' She
stamped her foot in real fury as his grin mocked
her. 'Sometimes I really hate you, you know that?
Just who the hell do you think you are?'

'Someone who's obeying his conscience against
his most basic instincts,' he replied. He studied her
body with hooded eyes. 'Do you think I don't
want to stay—and pursue this to its logical
conclusion?'

Suddenly aware of her nakedness, she turned
her back rudely on him. 'Mr Saintly,' she snapped.
But the meaning in his words had sobered her.

'Luckily,' he grinned, 'it's too dark to come out
with that cliché about you being beautiful when
you're angry.' He pulled her round, and peered at
her scowling face. 'In fact, it doesn't suit you a
bit.'

Her eyes hot with tears, she stamped off across
the sand to pull her dress on behind a convenient
dune. Sometimes she really *did* hate César
Levertov. She shrugged her wet body resentfully
into the golden silk. But her anger was already
ebbing away. Maybe it *was* a bit much to squirm
half-naked against a virile man like César, and
expect him to keep his passions under control.
And, tremblingly delicious though the thought of
César losing his control might be, she had to admit
that he'd shown fantastic self-discipline. And she'd
been so cross with him, ungrateful hussy that she

was. She hadn't exploded like that in years, and to tell the truth, she was almost relieved that she still had the capacity to do so. Further evidence, she thought wryly, of the regeneration of Lola Golightly.

'César, I'm sorry,' she said, coming up to join him as he buttoned his shirt. 'I didn't mean to sound so petulant.'

'It was quite a display,' he smiled, kissing her. 'You looked as though you were enjoying yourself.'

'Not exactly enjoying myself,' she said ruefully, snuggling against him as they walked back towards the car. 'Just letting off a lot of pent-up steam. And César——'

'Hmmm?'

'I don't *want* to thank you for stopping, but I guess I ought to. You're a lot more responsible then I am.'

'It hurts,' he admitted. His arm was warm around her, and not even the wet patches on her dress could interfere with her happiness now. 'It's simple, though. If we're to make love every time the urge takes us, then we really ought to be married.'

Lola was stunned into silence.

Married? The idea that he was joking made her glance up at his face quickly, but his expression was quite calm. Numbly, she stared ahead. Married. The word was still rolling around inside her brain like a boulder on an iron roof. Married to César Levertov. Yes, she'd thought about their relationship, and yes, she did love him. She knew that now. But in all her heart-searchings and speculations, the idea of marriage had never so much as crossed her mind.

She'd been wondering how to hold on to César for a matter of weeks, or months. Not in terms of a lifetime, not in terms of living in that bronze-lit villa with him, bearing his children, joining her own life to his for ever. God, the thought was immense, almost unfathomable. Marry César . . .

Suddenly she was terrified. Terrified that he didn't mean it, that it had simply been one of the careless things people say. And also terrified that he might have meant it after all. Terrified, that is, of the dazzling future that might be hers, the joy that could be waiting for her.

'You're very quiet,' he said gently as they drove along the deserted esplanade towards the city centre. 'Did I say something to upset you?'

'N-no,' she stammered, nestling down further into the Lamborghini's leather seats. She shot a glance at his face. Was there a smile on that passionate, superb mouth? She couldn't tell. Sometimes César could be the most impenetrable man, she realised wryly, and knew she was going to be left in an agony of doubt over that throw-away phrase. And knew that *he* knew, too.

'Good. I hope you're going to sleep well,' he went on, 'because I'm coming to pick you up before seven tomorrow.'

'I'll try,' she said drily.

'It's going to be a beautiful day,' César commented as they walked through the empty foyer of the Grande to his car early the next morning. 'Like the calm after a storm. Did you sleep well?'

'Very well,' she nodded, linking her arm tightly through his, and wondering whether he felt the same keen joy at seeing her as she felt at seeing him. 'I'm starving!'

'Breakfast later,' he promised. 'Business first.'

The early morning sun was casting long shadows across the busy streets as they cruised through the centre of the city. It was cool enough for Lola to have pulled on her quilted anorak, and she envied Mamie, still snugly asleep in the centrally heated suite. The morning air had washed away most of last night's tensions and blues, and she'd made up her mind to simply live for the present from now on—taking life without question for the next few days. Whether he had been serious or not last night, she would simply wait and see. That was logical, wasn't it?

The construction site was set among a group of glassy high-rise office buildings, overlooking the harbour; it was at present little more than the foundation, César explained, of what was to be a new business centre, funded by surplus profits from Aeromed's past two years' successes. The site itself was surrounded by a high green safety-fence.

As a precaution, César drove round the perimeter, checking for anything suspicious. The Lamborghini's engines were a fluttering growl in the quiet backstreets as the futuristic car nosed its way towards the car-parking area. It was too early for most of the workers to have arrived, though a few earthworking machines were already rumbling across the naked red earth as they parked the car. The site office, a long white Portacabin at the far end of the carpark, was deserted. Akhtopol had agreed to post the Aeromed tape in the letterbox here sometime during the previous day.

The early morning air was fresh and cool, and through the landscape of office-blocks Lola could see the sea glinting invitingly in the distance. There were butterflies in the pit of her stomach as they got out of the car and walked towards the office. Unlikely as it seemed, there was always a possibility that Akhtopol might have changed his mind, and not delivered the tape. He might even be lurking somewhere here, armed and waiting. She noticed that César's eyes were alert, probing the area for anything untoward. The same thoughts had evidently occurred to him, also. But his arm round her waist was deeply reassuring, and not a soul was stirring as they reached the office door without incident.

The letterbox which César had specified was set in the door of the Portacabin. He opened the door with his key to examine the contents of the wire tray behind. Lola's hart was pounding as he picked out the large brown envelope that was all the tray contained. He smiled at her, slightly tensely, and gave it to her.

She tore it open with shaky fingers. Inside was a chrome tape-disk. The label bore only the letters HVP.

'Herbert Victor Poincarré,' César supplied with a bitter expression. 'My erstwhile colleague.'

'Then it is the tape?' Lola asked.

'I think so,' he nodded. Their eyes met for a second. It was a strange moment, she thought. There was no sense of victory, only of relief. 'Well,' he said gently as he drew her to him, and hugged her, 'that seems to be that, little one. It only remains to give Akhtopol his tape back, and the comedy will be over.' His kiss was warm. *'Merci, Mademoiselle. Merci beaucoup.'*

She heaved a great sigh of happy relief. 'It's all over!'

'Almost,' he nodded. 'I don't trust friend Akhtopol any more now than before, though.' He thought hard for a few seconds, golden eyes intent. 'Can you drive, Lola?'

'Yes. Though I wouldn't like to try driving that thing,' she added, smiling at the low-slung Lamborghini.

'You'll manage. Listen to me. I want you to drive the car back to the villa now, and wait there for me.'

'But——'

'I've had the Cirrus tape put in my safe deposit,' he said, silencing her with a touch on her lips. 'When the bank opens I'll get it out, and deliver it to Akhtopol in person at the Grande.' He grinned at her expression. 'Don't worry, *chérie*. Akhtopol doesn't scare me, and I want to drive certain points home. In person.'

'You won't hurt him?' she pleaded urgently.

'I won't touch him,' he promised. 'But I want to make sure he won't bother you again. You understand,' he said gently. She nodded in silence. 'I'll be back by mid-morning. In the meantime, take the tape back to the villa.' He gave her the car keys, and a little electronic signalling device. 'That opens the gates. Lock yourself in, Lola. And have that breakfast I promised you.'

'I'll wait till you get back,' she decided, dropping the tape into her bag. She linked her arms round his neck, and looked up into his face, her eyes rainy-green. 'Take care, César. You're my whole life.'

'And you drive carefully,' he smiled. 'You know the route?'

'I think so.'

'*Bien*. It's not difficult.' He cupped her face in his hands, and kissed the corners of her mouth. 'I'll see you in two hours, little one.' He walked her to the car, and she slid gingerly into the bucket seat.

'I'm scared of this beast,' she confessed wryly.

'Just go easy on the gas. And remember to drive on the right!' The engine exploded into life as she twisted the key, and she engaged gear cautiously. *'Au revoir.'*

'See you,' she called. 'Be careful!'

Driving the Lamborghini was rather like sitting on a tiger's back. At the exit of the car park she looked back at his tall figure, and waved. Then she was heading through the crosstown traffic towards the *route nationale.*

She enjoyed the sunlit drive immensely. The car was a dangerous delight to drive, and she was just beginning to master it by the time she reached Cap-Ferrat. The villa was beautiful in the brilliant morning light, its white walls dazzling against the cobalt of the sea. The electric gates swung open in obedience to the pulsar César had given her, and Lola steered the unfamiliar car down the ramp that led into the cool underground parking-garage beneath the villa. The deep-throated engine was awesomely powerful, and she had to concentrate hard on keeping the accelerator under control. A delightful summery happiness was making her hum under her breath. What was she going to do until César's return? Explore the villa, simply laze on the patio, or perhaps wander along the beach, listening to the whispering wavelets on the shore . . . Hours of peaceful bliss stretched ahead.

The garage was empty but for the Range Rover that was César's second car, and dimly cool after the summer sun. She parked the Lamborghini next to the Range Rover, locked it, and walked towards the beechwood stairs that led up to the reception room.

Her heart almost stopped as he stepped out of the shadows.

A bulky man, coming towards her with slouching menace, infinitely threatening. She felt her mouth opening to scream as she recognised the pocked face and the small hot eyes. The man she'd seen with Akhtopol in the foyer, just before she'd entered his apartment.

'What do you want?' she whispered, her fingers crushing her bag to her breasts. Cradled almost negligently in the crook of his arm was a sub-machine-gun. A crude, brutal-looking thing with a skeletal fold-away stock. Screwed on to the snub muzzle was a heavy silencer. With the clarity of total shock she noticed that the weapon was used-looking, the matt black paint worn off on the rivets. As though he'd done this a hundred times before with the same gun and the same animal menace.

'Keep still,' he ordered roughly. He had a terrifying quality of being totally in command, of being ready to maim and kill without compunction. 'Where is the tape?'

Her throat frozen, she held out her bag. He tore it out of her hands, and emptied the contents on to the floor. He crouched quickly to scoop up the chrome disk, then tossed it aside contemptuously. 'Not this one! Where is the tape you stole from Akhtopol?'

'I—I don't know,' she stammered. 'I swear I don't! César's hidden it somewhere. He's going to send it back to Mr Akhtopol today!'

'Lying bitch. We will have it soon enough.' The words were almost casual. The muzzle of the sub-machine-gun didn't waver as he reached into the pocket of his cheap leather jacket, and withdrew a slim walkie-talkie radio set. He didn't speak into it, simply pressed the squawk button twice with his thumb, and put the set back into his pocket.

'Who are you?' she whispered, her throat dry. Reaction was making her body shake now, her heart pounding unevenly inside her. 'What do you want?'

'I'm going to leave a little message for Levertov,' he said softly, ignoring her shaky questions. 'Look. Listen. Learn.' Abruptly, he swung the sub-machine-gun away from her, and pressed the stock against his hip, squeezing the trigger.

The burst of fire was a compressed ripping sound that could barely have carried to the high beech hedge that lined the villa's well-tended grounds. But the effect was horrific. The gleaming Lamborghini she'd just stepped out of rocked madly on its suspension as the murderous hail tore through the steel bodywork, the windscreen and windows exploding into a million diamonds, two tyres bursting into shreds.

Lola screamed in terror, arms whipping up instinctively to protect her face from the flying glass and steel and brickwork. It lasted barely six or seven seconds, and then there was only a ringing silence and the bonfire-night stink of cordite.

White-faced, she lowered her arms slowly. The fifty-thousand pound car was hideously ravaged, its bodywork buckled and ripped by the bullets, the once-elegant bonnet yawning obscenely open. Oil was bleeding silently from beneath the engine.

'You're insane,' she said in numb disbelief,

turning to him with wide, dark eyes. The black muzzle was trained on her stomach again, and a surge of nausea accompanied the sudden realisation of what a similar burst would do to her own body.

He nodded once, slowly, as though reading her thoughts.

'Exactly. A lesson for him. And for you.' He smiled, showing square yellow teeth. 'It would give me great pleasure, little thief, to do to you what I have just done to your boyfriend's plaything.' He patted the gun. 'With this. Or with a knife. Or with my bare hands.' His eyes were greedy. 'Do you understand me?'

In a nightmare-like trance, Lola nodded without speaking. Her throat and mouth were dry as bone, the fear in her a silent, tearing scream that could find no outlet. Her knuckles were white, her body quivering with an unstoppable tremor, like a frightened dog's.

'Turn around,' Her legs felt oddly alien as she turned stiffly away, unsteady things that belonged to someone else. 'Walk to the door.' She obeyed, knowing that he'd be a pace behind her, the gun pointed unwaveringly at her spine.

Dear God, what was this? He could murder her right here and now if he wanted to. Her life in exchange for the stolen tape, was that what he was planning? But why hadn't he simply waited for César to send it back to Akhtopol? And why, in God's name, all this violence for the sake of a tape which contained nothing more than evidence of Akhtopol's fraud?

César! New terror reached for her heart as she suddenly imagined him arriving back at the villa for some reason, to fetch papers maybe—seeing her captor, trying to rescue her, his body being torn to pieces by that terrible compressed venom——

'Walk,' he said sharply, his voice cutting through the hysteria of her thoughts like a knife. As she walked up the ramp and into the sunlight, a car pulled up on the gravelled drive, a silver Volvo with tinted windows. The back door was thrown open, and the man behind her thrust her unceremoniously on to the plush seat with a hard hand, and climbed swiftly in beside her, slamming the door behind him.

Akhtopol was in the driving-seat. He slapped his door-button home, and the central locking system clicked the bolts of all the doors shut. Then gravel spurted beneath the tyres as the Volvo accelerated hard down the drive and towards the autoroute.

'Please,' Lola said in a tense voice, 'that tape will be returned to you by tomorrow, I promise——'

The man beside her touched the muzzle of the machine-gun to the swell of her left breast. It was an almost gentle movement—except for the black ring of powder-smudge that the mouth of the gun left against the crisp white linen of her dress. The words died in her throat.

'Unless you wish Levertov to find you floating in the sea, Miss Golightly, hold your tongue.' The silent scream surged in her throat again, unable to find release.

Akhtopol glanced over his shoulder quickly, fear bright in his black eyes.

'Have you hurt her?' he asked in a shaky voice.

'Relax, Ivanchik,' the other replied. There was a mocking note in his voice. 'Everything is under

control. I smashed the bastard's car for him.'
Exultation was bright in his black eyes.

'God, what for?' Akhtopol moaned, shifting
gear clumsily. They were driving towards the
mountains at five miles an hour less than the speed
limit. The car was new, the tinted glass ensuring
complete privacy.

'For an object lesson,' the man with the gun
smiled harshly. 'Just drive, and shut up.'

Dazedly, Lola realised that it had been a
ruthlessly efficient operation. Akhtopol was grey-
faced and clearly in terror, but the other worked
with the brutal efficiency of a professional. A
terrorist? A gangster? It was impossible to tell
which, or what his connection with Akhtopol was.
Only minutes had elapsed since she'd stepped out
of the Lamborghini. Within hours César was going
to discover she was gone—and see what had been
done to the car. The thought of what he would go
through brought tears swiftly to her eyes. The
ravaging of the car hadn't been intended simply to
frighten her, or to take a brutal revenge on César.
It had also been meant as a crudely direct message
for César, a cruel reminder of the ease with which
things—and people—could be shattered and
amputated. A warning to keep the authorities out
of this. She turned to glance at the man beside her,
her mouth twisting with disgust for people who
could behave like this.

'What are you?' she asked in a low voice. 'Some
kind of crazy political sect? Or just common
criminals?'

Akhtopol swung one arm clumsily over the seat,
his face glistening with sweat. His knuckles
cannoned roughly across her mouth, knocking her
face sideways.

'Slut,' he said. His voice was verging on hysteria as he turned back to the wheel. 'Shut your mouth. You've caused enough trouble.'

Stars were still exploding painfully inside her head as she explored her cut lip gingerly with the tip of her tongue, and tasted blood. Instinctively, she knew that the Bulgarian had only taken his own fear and tension out on her. The man with the gun simply shrugged, his expression unmoved.

The shrug didn't stir the unblinking black eye of the muzzle.

Lola lay back against the seat, shutting her eyes. Sickness and pain rose up inside her with a flood of sudden exhaustion. It occurred to her that Akhtopol was as frightened of the gunman as she was. Something had been terribly wrong with that tape, something that she and César had missed. With a strange fatalism she knew that it was very unlikely that she would come out of this alive. If only she could prevent César from coming near these people. Akhtopol lacked the courage, but the gunman would kill them both, she felt that instinctively.

Her fear, at least, was ebbing now. She could hate people who used terror and violence like this, hate and despise them. But she couldn't fear them, not now. Whatever fate awaited her, at least she would have that consolation. If only she could get that single message to César ... My love, she called out silently, willing the thought to somehow reach his mind, I'm not afraid any more. *I'm not afraid.*

They drove in silence for a quarter of an hour, meeting very little traffic on the country road. It occurred to Lola to wave frantically at the two or three oncoming cars they saw, but the tinted glass

would have made her practically invisible—and
the effort would have rewarded her with another
blow, or worse. She sat in silence, looking straight
ahead. Her shivering settled slowly into a tense
stillness, her mind struggling with the danger that
now faced her. How long would it be before the
alarm was raised?

Probably not until César got back to the villa.
By which time she would be miles away. What
were her chances of escape? The presence of the
man beside her was chilling. No chance at all.

The Volvo swung off the main road, and on to a
deserted-looking farm track. Lola's heart jolted
unpleasantly at the diversion. What was this? The
road to her prison? Her execution?

A mile and a half down the track a shabby little
farmstead stood half-hidden among trees. The few
patient French cows which stood in a knee-high
meadow added the perfect touch, and she
grimaced wryly despite her fear. A more innocent-
seeming place would be hard to find. Akhtopol
pulled up close to the front door, and switched off
the engine.

'This is the place, Yusif,' he said hoarsely.

'*Bravo.*' The gunman's voice was ironical. 'Get
out, Miss Golightly. We're home.'

CHAPTER EIGHT

'THIS is a mistake, a terrible mistake,' Akhtopol said for the tenth time. He was hunched up next to the telephone, gnawing at his big fingers in nervous tension. 'We should hov waited for Levertov. He would hov kept his bargain.'

'You are weak, Ivan. Weak and stupid. César Levertov is neither.' Yusif's eyes didn't leave Lola as he spoke. They'd made her sit among the rubbish on the floor with her hands folded in her lap, and the gunman's eyes had been undressing her greedily for the past three hours. 'The information on that tape could tie a noose round both our necks,' he went on. He studied Lola's breasts, and grinned. 'What do you say—shall we have some sport with the girl?'

'For God's sake!' Akhtopol stood up and took a few jerky paces round the room. Lola knew that Yusif's crude threats of rape were made as much to torment Akhtopol as to terrify her. Her hips were aching from the long hours of sitting on the hard floor, and she'd more than once been on the edge of fainting. She looked tiredly at the Bulgarian's bulky figure, and felt a twinge of compassion for him. His nerves were clearly as raw with suspense as her own. 'You should hov let me handle this in my own way, Yusif. He would never hov found the evidence of the Abdus deal—and by now the tape would be back in my apartment. This way——!' He made a helpless gesture, his rocky face pale. 'He is bound to suspect something, examine the tape in more detail——'

'It was lucky I found out your stupidity before it was too late.' Yusif spat on to the floor, and sent a glance of pure malice at the Bulgarian. 'Levertov's so-called arrangement was a trap. If I had not intervened, we would both now be in a French police cell.'

'But Levertov——'

'Don't worry about Levertov,' Yusif sneered. 'He is infatuated with this slut.' He gestured with the gun at where Lola squatted silently on the floor. 'He will be too terrified of her coming to any harm to do anything but what we order him to do. Believe me.' He dug in his pocket for a cigarette, the first he'd lit since the abduction this morning, and inhaled the pungent smoke luxuriously. 'Try again,' he ordered.

Akhtopol picked up the telephone, and dialled in silence. They had been ringing the same number—the number of César's villa—every ten minutes for the past two hours. The image of César's bronzed face rose up, achingily sharp, in her mind. Was he back now, waiting by the telephone like a leopard coiled to spring? She felt her own nerves stretching as the pause lengthened, and her whole body flinched involuntarily as Akhtopol slammed the receiver down.

'No answer.' There was a note of desperation on his face. 'He's not back. Let me go back to the Grande, Yusif. The tape will be there, I know it.'

'So will the French security police. We stay.' The blunt authority was enough to silence the Bulgarian. Yusif had the manners and ruthlessness of an irregular soldier. A sergeant-major, Lola found herself guessing, in some guerilla army.

His connection with Akhtopol was slowly becoming clear to her. From what she'd picked up in snatches of talk between the two men, it seemed that Akhtopol had been negotiating with the man called Yusif to supply him with some items known as R3710s. This information, recorded somewhere on the tape she'd stolen from Akhtopol's suite, was apparently highly secret, and potentially explosive. Her dark green eyes followed Yusif as he rose, and thrust the gun into Akhtopol's unwilling arms.

'I'm going to relieve my bladder. Watch her.' He poked his cigarette into Akhtopol's mouth, laughed sharply at the Bulgarian's expression, and stamped out. Akhtopol sank into his seat, holding the weapon awkwardly on his lap. Their eyes met, and she saw the fear lurking in Akhtopol's unsteady gaze.

'Please,' she said in a low voice, 'what's this all about? You and César came to a deal. Why did you break it?'

'I did *not* break this deal. If your friend and I had been left to work our problems out in our own way, we would all now be drinking champagne.' He gestured at the door Yusif had just walked through. '*He* was the one who interfered, with all his violence, his terrorist ways. Pig!' He threw the cigarette on to the floor, and ground it out. His voice became a spiteful whine. 'When he found out, look what he did to me.' He pulled his shirt clumsily open. Akhtopol's rocky appearance, Lola realised suddenly, was an illusion. He was flabby, his body heavy with lard. Across the flaccid skin of his chest were big violet bruises. 'He hit me,' Akhtopol said, almost in disbelief. 'His partner.

He *hit* me. But for him, none of this would have happened.'

Lola looked away as Akhtopol buttoned his shirt again, and felt nausea rise in her throat. Dear God. Dear God, what was going to become of them? 'Is he going to kill César?' she asked tautly.

'He will kill us all!' Akhtopol lowered his anguished voice to a frightened whisper. 'He will kill you and Levertov once he has the tape, and then he will kill me!'

'Then you must stop him,' Lola said urgently, leaning forward to try and get her message across to the frightened Bulgarian. 'Don't let him do this!'

'What can I do?' He twisted his bulky shoulders in an age-old shrug of fatalism.

'Call the police now!' Lola hissed. 'Hold the gun on him when he comes back.'

'I am a businessman.' His mouth was weak, his eyes almost tearful. 'Yusif is a Colonel in the Cyren Freedom Army. He would take the gun away from me in a second. And then he would torment us both.'

Lola opened her mouth to argue further, but the Bulgarian pointed the gun shakily at her, naked fear on his face. 'Shut your mouth! He will hear you!'

'Why is he doing this?' Lola asked quietly. She shifted stiffly, trying to ease her agonised hips. 'What's so important on that tape?'

'Helicopters.' Akhtopol was gnawing at his fingers again, and Lola saw that the skin round the blunt nails was bitten raw. 'R3710 helicopters for the Cyren Freedom Army,' he said almost absently. 'I curse the day that ever I met Yusif and listened to his proposal.'

'Are they terrorists?' Lola asked.

'Terrorists?' Akhtopol gave a ghastly smile. 'You hov not heard of Cyren? These people train the world's terrorist forces, my friend. The IRA, the Red Brigades. Baader-Meinhoff—all have been trained at Colonel Yusif's camps in the desert. He teaches them to kill and maim and sabotage.' He shuddered, closing his eyes. 'Devils teaching other devils the tricks of hell.'

'But surely Cirrus would never sell helicopters to someone like that?' Lola probed, curiosity overcoming her exhaustion for a moment. A tired, wordly wise look crossed Akhtopol's face.

'Of course not. But Cirrus would sell helicopters to six or seven innocent sources. Sources acting as a front for Colonel Yusif.'

'Is that what you and he had been planning?' she gasped.

'Yes,' Akhtopol sighed. 'Yes, yes. Helicopters for Yusif. A few false papers, some imaginary companies—and a big profit for Ivan Akhtopol.'

'And what will Yusif do with the helicopters?' Lola asked in fascinated horror.

'Kill,' Akhtopol shrugged. 'The R3710 is very versatile. They can be equipped to take rockets, machine-guns, mines, who knows what projects he has in mind.' He looked away from Lola's horrified expression. 'It was business. Purely business.'

'And the details of the deal are on that tape?' she pressed.

'All the details,' Akhtopol nodded. He was staring at the gun in his arms as though it were something utterly new to him. 'When you stole that tape, you did not know what you were doing, Miss Golightly. I tried to hide the theft from

Yusif, because I knew how he would react—but when he discovered what had happened, he went crazy. He said we had to take immediate action——'

'Action?' Yusif sneered at the Bulgarian from the doorway. 'What do you know about action, Ivanchik?' He swaggered across to Akhtopol, and held out his hand. 'Stick to capitalism, my friend. Give me the gun.'

Ivan Akhtopol hesitated. A sudden flare of mingled hope and fear electrified Lola. Was he going to stand up to the terrorist? Yusif's face tightened with anger.

'Akhtopol—the gun.' But Akhtopol's own face was now white and set. Holding the weapon awkwardly, he stumbled to his feet and backed away from Yusif.

'This has gone far enough, Yusif,' he quavered. 'I'm going to the Grande to pick up that tape, and I'm taking the girl with me——'

'Idiot.' The terrorist stalked towards him, murder in his eyes. Frozen with terror, Lola could only watch. 'You dare to point a gun at me—a corrupt little salesman like you!'

'Yusif, please,' Akhtopol begged, desperation making his voice crack, 'let's end this now.'

'Weakling.' Yusif moved fast, tearing the weapon out of Akhtopol's grasp. Lola's heart sank bitterly, and she closed her eyes as he slapped Akhtopol hard across the face. 'It will end soon enough,' he promised grimly, checking the gun. 'For you as well as for——'

He didn't finished the sentence. The window behind them exploded into fragments with an eardrum-splitting crash, and two figures in khaki burst through it. Lola didn't even have time to scream. Choking white smoke swirled through the room. There was a yelled command in French, and she cowered back into the corner. Yusif was still whirling to face the intruders, his gun tightening against his hip, when the door was smashed inwards and more men hurled themselves into the room, making him glance sideways in shock. The terrorist's hesitation was fatal. Two big bodies slammed into him, flattening him against the wall, and a soldier, his face blackened with paint, ripped the weapon out of his fingers. Akhtopol, like Lola, was cowering against the wall, covering his head. Yusif, shouting savagely in his own language, was struggling like a wild beast.

Someone hit him hard, and they kicked his legs out from under him. He lapsed into stillness, both arms pinioned, glowering at the guns that were trained on him.

Bewilderment didn't stop Lola's tears of pure relief. One of the men who'd smashed their way in through the window raised his weapon, and ran to her side, helping her to her feet with gentle hands.

'Chérie——' She looked up into César's face, and melted into his strong arms with a sob. Firmly, he led her outside, her faltering steps crunching on broken glass. The house seemed to be full of soldiers, and in the brilliant sunshine outside, four olive-green Jeeps were pulling up.

'Are you hurt?' he asked urgently.

'N-no,' she sobbed. 'Oh my darling, I've been so f-frightened——' He crushed her to him, the unfamiliar camouflage uniform he wore rough against her wet cheek.

'The army let me go in with them,' he told her. 'I don't think they could have stopped me, anyway. At first I couldn't see you, in all the

smoke and confusion. I was going to kill him if
he'd——'

'No,' she pleaded, holding her hand against his
mouth. 'Don't say it.'

'It's finished now,' he said huskily.

She nodded her head, seemingly unable to stem
her tears. He let her cry them out, cradling her
against him in the warmth of the afternoon.

'There is a God, after all,' he said softly. 'I've
been praying all morning that I'd find you safe.'

She clung to him, the smell of wild thyme and
geraniums strong in her nostrils. The nightmare
was over. Only the wonderful reality of César's
arms remained, close and safe and strong around
her.

'How did you find me?' she asked, when her
shaking had begun to subside a little.

'Through the telephone at the villa.' He led her
gently to a bench, and she collapsed on to it,
gratefully sinking back into his arms. 'I went back
to the villa very soon after you'd left Nice, and
saw the car.' He grimaced. 'I nearly died when I
thought you might be still inside it. Then I called
the security police at once. They'd had information
that an important terrorist called Yusif was in
Nice, and they'd been trying to track him down.
They connected him with your kidnapping
immediately, and they connected a special device
to the telephone, a machine able to trace calls
within seconds. I didn't even have to pick the
telephone up. After the first call, at ten, they went
into immediate action.' He brushed the golden hair
away from her pale face, and kissed her eyelids
tenderly. 'Feeling better?'

'Yes,' she nodded. The lines of his face, gentled
now with love, fascinated her, as though his was

the first face she'd ever seen, on the dawn of history. 'Akhtopol was going to sell him helicopters,' she said.

'So it seems,' César smiled. 'Mr Akhtopol is a very dishonest and foolish little man. He's lucky Yusif didn't kill him.'

'He was going to kill us all,' she said, the memory of the horror darkening her eyes.

'He'll never kill again,' César said grimly. 'The French Justice Department will see to that.' She followed his gaze to the farmhouse door. Yusif, and then Akhtopol, pleading in French with his captors, were being hustled out of the farmhouse fast, and into a closed van. Beyond them, in the field, the cows hadn't even stopped chewing. High above, in the blue dome of the sky, a helicopter was hovering like a skylark.

An officer was coming towards them, looking extremely satisfied with the morning's work.

'Don't let me go,' she begged.

'Let you go?' César smiled tenderly. 'I'm never going to let you go, Lola. I love you, don't you know that by now? I love you, little burglar. I always will.'

The officer, being French, stopped in mid-stride, turned his back, and waited for them to part. There was a broad smile on his face, and he didn't seem to mind having to wait a long time.

Later, in the back of the military car heading for Nice, she raised her head from his chest as a thought struck her. 'Your poor car,' she said. 'It was horrible what he did to it . . .'

'To hell with the car,' he smiled. He reached into his pocket, and tugged out a silver hip-flask. 'Not medically recommended,' he said, uncorking it, 'but I think you've recovered enough from your

shock to benefit from it.' The cognac burned like
fire in her throat, but she felt its strength
counteracting the horrible weakness in her stomach. 'They could have destroyed everything I had,'
he went on, watching her drink, 'so long as you
were unharmed.' He touched her cheek, a
wondering look in his eyes. 'I've been too
preoccupied with material things, Lola. For a long
time now. Friend Yusif taught me a lesson today,
a lesson I'll never forget—that love is the most
important thing of all.'

'Yusif taught you that?' she said, smiling
unsteadily. He took the flask from her, and corked
it. 'You know what my life has been like,' he said
slowly, burshing the tangle of her hair into golden
order. 'I never had much of a family, never really
had anyone to care for except myself. I've always
let other things come first—my factory, my career,
my designs.' He smiled. 'My damned Churchill.
God above, when I think how your life has been
risked for the sake of that senseless hunk of
aluminium, I think I must have been more than
half-mad.'

'You're brilliant, César.' She rubbed her cheek
against his hand, feeling the long hours of tension
uncurling and drifting into peace inside her. 'And
brilliant people are always dedicated to their
work.'

'Not to the exclusion of the people they love
most.' He kissed her mouth with infinite tenderness. 'I have a confession to make. I've never really
known how to deal with you, Lola Golightly.' He
shook his head in response to her incredulous
smile. 'No. It's true. You've always affected me
much, much more deeply than I ever wanted to
recognise. I've tried to make light of it, always

tried to keep you at bay. I'll never do so again.
Not any more. It's all yours, Lola. Everything I've
created, everything I've built, everything I am.
Yours for ever.'

'I only want you.' She kissed him, not caring
that she was breathing cognac rather tipsily all
over him. Suddenly the entire world was flooded
with sun. 'I love you.'

The autumn morning was so warm that the
dozens of white rosebuds in the bouquet were
beginning to open among the sprays of fern, and
their sweet fragrance filled the car. Chris
Golightly held his daughter's gloved hand tight,
and smiled at her.

'Even your mother wasn't more beautiful than
you are today, Lola,' he said quietly. The swathes
of white silk around her hips rustled as she leaned
across to hug him tight. He was magnificent in his
morning-suit, this reserved father of hers. More
than once over the past few weeks—it was now
almost two months since that terrible morning at
the farmhouse—she'd caught mistiness in those
cool blue eyes. They were misty now, she could see
that through the veil, and a lump was in her own
throat as she brushed some imaginary dust from
his immaculate lapels.

'You really like him?' she asked, a little shakily.

'I think he's wonderful. And he adores you.' He
grinned suddenly. 'How a scamp like you managed
to catch a man like César I'll never know. I only
wish Zara was here to see this.' He looked up at
the cloudless Mediterranean sky for a second, then
turned to her, more hesitant. 'Lola, I haven't been
the father I should have been. To you and Tom I
must have seemed so cold sometimes. I always

found it difficult to express my innermost feelings——'

'Oh, Dad,' she said, 'I understand.'

'Zara's death made me worse than ever,' he said. 'You understand that, too, I know. She was so much better than I am at expressing things. But I want you to know that my love for you and Tom has always been there, strong and deep.'

'I never doubted that, Dad. Nor did Tom.' How silver his hair was now; it made him look even more distinguished, more imposing. She was so proud of him, almost as proud as he obviously was of her!

He adjusted the exquisite lace of her veil carefully, and went on, 'César's love will be your life now, girl. You and César will have children of your own soon. Don't make the same mistakes. Stay close to them, always.'

'We will,' she promised gently.

'He really is a wonderful man,' he said, his face still serious. 'I trust him implicitly. Be true to him, Lola, the way your mother was to me.' She nodded, and the twinkle crept into his blue eyes again. 'Okay, lecture over. And on your wedding-day, too. Just don't take too long in giving me a grandchild!'

Colour touched her cheeks as she shook her head, smiling. This happiness inside her was almost like a child, growing and swelling to maturity against her heart. Too real to be a dream, almost too beautiful to be true, her life was opening like these rosebuds on her lap. Opening and expanding in the southern sun.

At the villa now, in the sea-filled peace, the long tables were waiting for the guests to return, their burden of wine, bread, roasts and fruit, and the most stunning wedding-cake Lola had ever seen in the centre of everything, carefully watched over by the waiters. I am like that table, she thought suddenly. Loaded with the autumn harvest of richness. Like the altar and its more-precious burden, laden with flowers and the good things that the world has to offer. So lucky, so fulfilled.

How could all this have happened to me? I didn't deserve it, I didn't . . .

Luck—or providence—had played such an important part in her story! The potential for tragedy had been so great, and yet the outcome had been so happy. Well, she thought, happy for some. She and César had played a minor role in the trial of Akhtopol and Yusif the month before. Both had received heavy sentences for conspiracy, among other things. Poor Akhtopol, a corrupt businessman who had simply had his finger in too many pies, had been dealt with more leniently than the terrorist leader, who had faced dozens of other serious charges.

'Your tan makes you look so much like Zara,' her father said, interrupting her memories as he touched her hand. 'You've got more Mediterranean in you than I thought!'

She laughed softly. She and César had spent so many days in the sun together, lost in one another, that their skins had been bronzed to deep mahogany. And in the peace of the summer's end their love had grown and gathered strength.

She'd rebuked him once, while they were planning the wedding, for keeping her waiting so long. 'You know how hungry I am for your love,' she'd complained. 'I reckon you must enjoy dangling me on a string!'

'Sometimes,' he'd replied, 'I think I never knew

what love was till you.' His lips had been like
velvet against hers. 'I was only half-alive, I think.
You make me a man, Lola. You give me life . . .'

She was dreamy-eyed with thought as the Rolls-
Royce cruised silently down the tree-lined avenue.
The cathedral was in sight now, a pyramid of
honey-coloured stone rising up against the cobalt
of the sea. She raised her veil to kiss her father
once, quickly, on the cheek, and five minutes later
the chauffeur was opening the door for them. The
bridesmaids were already waiting outside, ready to
flutter round her and adjust the ravages done to
her dress by the car-journey.

Then all was ready.

The swell of the organ was deep and beautiful as
her father tucked her hand under his arm, smiling
at her with that mist in his eyes again, and led her
slowly up the aisle, under the vast stone arches
above.

The vast nave was crowded with people. Where
had they all come from? Many were strangers to
her, though she recognised several of the soldiers
in the back pews. The Misses Jenkins, both
already snuffling into handkerchiefs, peeped at her
eagerly as she passed by. Little 'Aaahs' and
'Ooohs' rustled among the congregation as people
sneaked sideways glances. The large group of her
girlfriends, however, conspicuous by their youthful
clothing, craned their necks shamelessly to see her.
Her heart was brimming over already, and she had
to lean hard on her father's arm as they made their
way towards the scarlet carpet at the foot of the
altar.

'You look *ravishing*,' Mamie Prenderghast
hissed as she passed by. Her hat, a vast bowl of
artificial fruit, dominated every other hat in the

cathedral, a galleon among coracles. Vivien Roche, beside her, twittered with delight. In the next pew, Baroness Var was leaning on her two sticks, her face wearing a strange, dreamy smile. She nodded to Lola, quietly. Hers had been the most beautiful wedding-present of all, a silver tea-service from the chateau, glowing with an almost ethereal light.

And then she was at the altar. Tom was looking as nervous as a boy at César's side. He smiled unsteadily at her, immaculate in his best man's suit. She smiled back.

And at last raised her eyes to César's. The golden light in his gaze was calm, deep with love. The memories blazed up in her mind—the burglar, all in black, dropping through the hotel window; the taste of his lips in the sunset; scrambling over Akhtopol's wall in the rain; the explosive relief of the rescue; all the strange events that had led her to this man and this marriage . . .

The touch of his hand was warm. It stopped her trembling at once, stilling her mind and welding it to his. That extraordinary sense of unity between them was instant. This was the way it would always be, she knew. A love deeper than any understanding, no longer darkened with doubt or clouded with fear.

You give me life.

She couldn't tear her eyes away from his for a long moment. Then he smiled quietly, and nodded gently towards the priest, waiting patiently in front of them, Obediently, she looked up at the priest's young face, feeling the strength of her husband's body against her side, and waited to say the words that would change her life forever.

ANNE MATHER

Anne Mather, one of Harlequin's leading romance authors, has published more than 100 million copies worldwide, including **Wild Concerto**, a *New York Times* best-seller.

Catherine Loring was an innocent in a South American country beset by civil war. Doctor Armand Alvares was arrogant yet compassionate. They could not ignore the flame of love igniting within them... whatever the cost.

HIDDEN IN THE FLAME

Get this book FREE!

Mail to:
Harlequin Reader Service

In the U.S.	In Canada
2504 West Southern Ave.	P.O. Box 2800, Postal Station A
Tempe, AZ 85282	5170 Yonge St., Willowdale, Ont. M2N 6J3

YES! I want to be one of the first to discover **Harlequin American Romance.** Send me FREE and without obligation *Twice in a Lifetime.* If you do not hear from me after I have examined my FREE book, please send me the 4 new **Harlequin American Romances** each month as soon as they come off the presses. I understand that I will be billed only $2.25 for each book (total $9.00). There are no shipping or handling charges. There is no minimum number of books that I have to purchase. In fact, I may cancel this arrangement at any time. *Twice in a Lifetime* is mine to keep as a FREE gift, even if I do not buy any additional books.

154 BPA BPGE

Name _____ (please print)

Address _____ Apt. no.

City _____ State/Prov. _____ Zip/Postal Code

Signature (If under 18, parent or guardian must sign.)

AMR-SUB-2R

Harlequin

Tender, captivating stories that sweep to faraway places and delight with the magic of love.

Exciting romance novels for the woman of today — a rare blend of passion and dramatic realism.

Sensual and romantic stories about choices, dilemmas, resolutions, and above all, the fulfillment of love.

GEN-A-2

Harlequin is romance...

INDULGE IN THE PLEASURE OF SUPERB ROMANCE READING BY CHOOSING THE MOST POPULAR LOVE STORIES IN THE WORLD

Longer, more absorbing love stories for the connoisseur of romantic fiction.

Contemporary romances— uniquely North American in flavor and appeal.

An innovative series blending contemporary romance with fast-paced adventure.

and you can never have too much romance.

Experience the warmth of . . .

Harlequin Romance

**The original romance novels.
Best-sellers for more than 30 years.**

Delightful and intriguing love stories
by the world's foremost writers
of romance fiction.

Be whisked away to dazzling
international capitals . . .
or quaint European villages.
Experience the joys of falling in love . . .
for the first time, the best time!

Harlequin Romance

**A uniquely absorbing journey
into a world of superb romance reading.**

Wherever paperback books are sold, or through
Harlequin Reader Service

In the U.S.
2504 West Southern Avenue
Tempe, AZ 85282

In Canada
P.O. Box 2800, Postal Station A
5170 Yonge Street
Willowdale, Ontario M2N 5T5

**No one touches the heart of a woman
quite like Harlequin!**